THE WILD DOG
OF EDMONTON

OTHER BOOKS BY

DAVID GREW

The Wild Dog of Edmonton
Whitepaw Goes North
(A sequel to THE WILD DOG OF EDMONTON)
Beyond Rope and Fence
The Ghost Mare

*Dwight looked down at mother and baby
silently.*

THE
Wild Dog
OF EDMONTON

By David Grew

Illustrated by
ELLEN SEGNER

Grosset & Dunlap
NEW YORK

CONTENTS

ILLUSTRATIONS

THE WILD DOG OF EDMONTON

CHAPTER I

Being Born

IT WAS the first of February. The half-prairie, half-forest country along the North Saskatchewan River, a hundred and fifty miles east of Edmonton, was still in the grip of the Canadian winter. The Burnell farmyard, hacked out of one of the many patches of poplar woods which broke up the flat, prairie spaces of the northern half of Alberta, consisted of a small log-cabin house and a much better-looking red barn with a silvery gray roof.

It was a bright, sunny day, as some of northwest Canada's coldest days often are, and the surface of the snows had been sparkling smilingly. The eaves had dripped a little, at noon, the drops beating out a jagged trough in the snow directly below them.

As the early winter evening approached, the sunny smiling of the day began fading away, turning into a cold seriousness. The temperature began to fall. The dripping at the eaves froze into long, sharp icicles, and a cold sadness lowered over the country. But the little log cabin, in the midst of it all, was beginning to glow with the light which gleamed through its small, polished windows, with its white, starched curtains, proclaiming that exciting state of things—company coming.

The door of the log cabin opened, and a fairly tall, lanky boy of about fourteen came out, carrying a huge bundle of bedclothes under one arm and an unlighted lantern in the other. A woman's voice followed him out: "Don't dirty yourself all up out there, now."

Dwight shut the door behind him and started slowly toward the barn, walking a bit stiffly, because his newly-washed overalls had shrunk and were tucked a bit too tightly into his felt boots. His sandy hair, under the visor of his fur-lined cap, was wet and plastered down. His blue eyes, large and round, sparkled with anticipation; but the starched shirt collar under his sheepskin coat had already rubbed his neck red. When he reached the woodpile in the center of the yard, he set his lantern down, and sliding a finger between collar and neck, puckered and twisted his lips in silent protest.

Towser, a reddish, part-collie dog, leaped out joyfully from the other side of the woodpile; and Nip, the black shepherd dog, came bounding toward him from the barn.

"You fellows keep down, now," warned Dwight. "Don't want y'ur dirty paws on me, t'night."

Both dogs stopped a few feet off; and when Dwight lumbered on, started after him, ears pricked, puzzled. Near the barn doorway, Dwight stopped again. He had suddenly caught sight of something moving slowly along the top of the snowdrift which lay against the haystack, to the side of him. Babsie, the third of the Burnell dogs, was coming down the incline with the slow, labored tread of an invalid.

Dwight watched her come a few seconds then whistled to her. He saw her stop, look up toward him, then turn and slink away, down the other side of the drift.

He was about to whistle again, when he heard the distant jingle of sleigh bells, and immediately plunged into the barn.

Across the entire length of the barn he ran, tearing up the broad stairway, three steps at a time. In the hayloft above, in the half-darkness, he dropped his bundle of bedclothes on the hay, lighted his lantern and hung it up on a nail. Taking the pitchfork which was standing there, he tore masses of hay from the huge pile, packed into the loft, and spread it out into a thick, flat layer on the floor, some ten feet away from the homemade stove which John Burnell had fashioned out of an old gasoline drum.

Right over the hay, he spread a horse blanket; and on top of that, he laid his three blankets with his pillow under the two with which he was to cover himself. On top of all this he spread another horse blanket, reinforcing that with all the gunny sacks he could gather up from the hayloft floor.

He was as much thrilled about being able to sleep up there in the hayloft by himself as he was about the coming of the new schoolteacher. He loved that hayloft, especially on winter nights, when he could build a cozy fire and withdraw by himself to where nobody could find fault with him, nor keep telling him how he ought to act. He liked to think of it as his very own room. At the orphan asylum, in Edmonton, he had had to sleep in a dormitory with dozens of other youngsters. And in the log cabin with the Burnells, his bed was separated from the Burnell bed and the rest of the one big room of the cabin, only by curtains.

He was piling on the empty sacks at the foot of his bed when he heard the sleigh bells come jingling into the yard. Quickly turning out the lantern, so that his foster father would not know he was up there, he made his way to the window facing the yard.

He blew his breath on one of the small, frost-covered panes and melted an opening with his hot breath, to look through. There was still some light in the wintry evening outdoors, and he saw John Burnell jump from his seat on the sleigh box and start unhooking the horses. The teacher, who had been sitting beside him, with a robe wrapped completely around her, threw the robe back and carefully lowered herself to the snow, as if she were half frozen.

Dwight could barely make out the faint glow of her face when, at the rear of the sleighbox, she pulled at some of her belongings. Her rather small, slender form surprised him. He had expected a big, fat woman, like the last teacher they had had.

Dwight wanted to go down there and help, but he hesitated. He was very backward about meeting new people. He didn't know just what he ought to say to the teacher. While he hesitated, John Burnell unhooked the horses and sent them by themselves to the barn, and he himself followed the schoolteacher to the house. At the cabin door, Dwight heard him ask his wife where Dwight was.

Dwight then got his lantern and hurrying down to the barn below, hung it up and proceeded to remove the harness from the horses who had gone to their own stalls. He was hanging up the last bit of harness when his foster father came back into the barn.

"Where y'u been?" he demanded. "Afraid o' the schoolma'am?"

"Up in the hayloft, fixin' m' bed," muttered Dwight.

"Don't feed the horses too much oats," said Burnell. "Run out o' feed an' there won't be money to buy any more. An' y'u better not give 'em water till after supper. They're pretty well het up, pullin' all day long on the hard snow roads."

The big farmer looked about the barn critically, noting that the stalls were clean and the mangers filled with hay. But he didn't praise Dwight for having done his chores well. John Burnell expressed himself only when things were not done well enough to suit him. He walked out silently.

Dwight dallied around as long as he dared, to postpone the ordeal of meeting the new teacher, in spite of the fact that he was rather anxious to see what she was like. Then, hanging up the lantern near the door where he would be able to find it easily in the dark, he blew it out and started with fast-beating heart for the cabin.

Near the cabin door, he brushed himself off and stamped the snow from his feet. Finally opening the door, his heart now thumping up in his neck, he entered as quietly as possible.

The one big room which served as kitchen, dining room and living room, was bright and cozy. The window curtains, clean and starched, reflected the light of the two kerosene lamps. The table, already set for dinner, sparkled and steamed. The cook stove, under a forest of pots, glowed red with heat, and a delightful warmth poured out of it.

The new schoolma'am was seated on a rocker beside the air-tight heater at the other end of the room, on the other side of the table. Her round, ruddy face was set off by a lacy, frill-like collar around her neck, and her wavy light-brown hair reflected the lamplight. The interest with which her sharp, blue eyes were fixed on him, flustered him; and he turned to the washbowl on the ledge near the door.

He washed his hands very slowly, and even more slowly dried them on the hanging towel; but when he finally attempted another look in her direction, she was still studying him, even as she was conversing with John Burnell.

The big farmer was sitting on the opposite side of the heater, "speechifying" as his wife called his grandiloquent manner, on "learnin' " and wheat-raising, his big feet reaching halfway into the room. He wore a plaid blazer, open at the neck, and his wrinkled throat stuck out of it like a leather boot. On his wind-parched face, covering his usually angry look, was his company smile.

Dwight sneaked up to a chair in the corner and quietly sat down.

"Why don't y'u shake hands with Miss Martinby?" asked Burnell, looking at Dwight as if he were disgusted with him. "Don't act's though y'u never saw nobody."

Dwight's cheeks went hot. With that introduction it was harder than ever for him to face the new teacher. With month after month going by without a stranger

coming to that lonely little homestead, he had had very
little practice in how to act before strangers.

Fortunately Mrs. Burnell, who had been too busy
dashing back and forth from stove to table to hear
what was going on, called out:

"Supper's ready now."

While Dwight was hesitating, afraid to look in her
direction, Miss Martinby got up and coming toward
him, smilingly extended her hand.

Dwight grinned sheepishly, as he shook hands with
her, nodding and mumbling what he thought he ought
to say; and they took their places at the table, the three
of them, Mrs. Burnell still fluttering about the stove.
John Burnell turned his head, when he was settled, and
looked at his wife impatiently. She understood at once
what he wanted and hurried over to her seat, sitting
down on the edge of it, the cloth with which she handled
hot dishes still in her hand. There she lowered her head
and closed her eyes tight.

John Burnell bowed his head till his chin threatened
to make a hole in his chest; and in a voice, ringing with
deep feeling, he asked the blessing, adding a lot of things,
Dwight thought, which he didn't usually say, for the
benefit of the schoolma'am, finishing finally with a re-
sounding "Amen." Then he immediately proceeded to
load up his plate, passing things to the teacher when he
was through serving himself.

As usual when a visitor was at the Burnell table, the
big farmer monopolized the conversation, while his silent, work-worn wife fluttered nervously back and
forth between the stove and the table. Dwight only half

heard what was being said, busy, all through the meal, thinking of the good times he would have in school for the next ten months.

"You didn't have any school here last year, did you?" he heard Miss Martinby ask.

"Couldn't get no teacher," Burnell shot back, defensively. "It's a chore tryin' t' keep school agoin' in this country. Most teachers won't come out this far from the railroad station. Winters here can be mighty bad, an' most folks are afraid t' send young ones four an' five miles t' school with maybe a blizzard comin' on before they can get back home. Because o' that, we got t' keep school open when we can, summer'n all, when we do get hold of a teacher. But in the summer time, a man needs 'is kids t' help. Farmers in this country can't afford t' hire help."

"He's makin' excuses to 'er, t' keep me out o' school soon's spring seedin' starts," thought Dwight. But he recalled that the school board had promised John Burnel that, since Dwight was the biggest boy attending school this year, he would be made the school janitor. Burnell would be obliged to let him go to school every day, if he was to be the janitor.

After the plain, country meal, Dwight helped Mrs. Burnell with the dishes; and, occasionally glancing at the teacher, he felt that she was pleased to see him help. When the dishes were done, Dwight sat back a little from the air-tight heater, looking at Miss Martinby when he dared, listening to the conversation but often wandering away in his own mind to imaginary scenes at the schoolhouse. Suddenly a belligerent tone in the farmer's voice aroused his attention.

"What gets me," John Burnell was saying, "is how them fool lawmakers in Edmonton sit around, holdin' down fine office chairs, tellin' us farmers what's best for our kids. I believe in education, same as the next fellow, but there ain't no use spendin' time an' money tryin' t' educate them's jes' ain't got the head t' learn."

"If we didn't have a compulsory attendance law, Mr. Burnell," said Miss Martinby, "some poor youngsters wouldn't even get the chance to show whether they have the head to learn or not."

"When a young one shows plain he weren't made f'r book-learnin', there ain't no sense keepin' 'im in school," argued Burnell. "It'd be much better t' let 'im work in the fields, where he c'n earn what it costs t' feed an' clothe 'im." He pointed a gnarled finger at Dwight. "Here's this boy. He'll go t' school till he's twenty, an he won't pass that eighth grade examination."

"That ain't fair!" cried Dwight, shame burning in his eyes. "Y'u kept me out o' school half the time—no school at all, last year!"

"You better keep your mouth shut," warned Mrs. Burnell in an undertone from where she was darning at the table.

"That's the thanks I get f'r takin' 'im out o' the asylum," said the farmer contemptuously.

"Some of the finest men that ever lived have done poorly in school," said Miss Martinby, an impatient frown on her forehead. "Sometimes it is only because they failed to understand some one thing or another.

Straightened out properly, Dwight may do splendidly."

Dwight was filled with gratification. She had taken his part. For her sake he would study as he had never studied in his life before. He would show Burnell that he had as good a head as anyone.

But if Dwight felt that he had the teacher on his side, he was too wise to gloat over it openly. He sat there silently, looking at the red-hot sides of the heater, imagining himself explaining in detail to Miss Martinby why he had done so poorly with the last teacher.

"Well, I guess you're as tired as I am, an' want t' get t' bed," said Burnell abruptly, rising.

"Good night, Miss Martinby," said Dwight shyly, not daring to look right at her, going straight for the door.

"Good night, Dwight," returned Miss Martinby. "Don't you worry about school. You'll find out that it's really very easy."

Dwight smiled triumphantly and looked up at her a second, helplessly. Then he made his way out, feeling that he should have said something, to show how much he appreciated her kindness.

Outdoors, the deep blue sky was ablaze with millions of sharp, sparkling stars; and the light, reflected from the broad stretches of hard, cold snow, produced a sort of moonlit effect. Every little thing, frozen into the hard crusts, had its shadow and looked like something watching him, as he trudged happily toward the barn door.

Near the barn door, Dwight caught sight of Babsie, again trying to climb up the snowdrift, to her hidden nest in the haystack. She was only halfway up, when she heard him and crouched down in her tracks, as if she had dropped there from exhaustion. This was where he had seen her when he had first heard the sleigh bells of John Burnell's return with the new school teacher.

"Gosh!" he cried to himself. "You ain't been up there all that time, Babsie, have y'u?"

Regarding her a moment from the distance, he started cautiously up the drift, toward her.

"Matter, Babsie?" he asked feelingly, as he approached her.

Babsie looked up at him and feebly wagged her tail.

Dwight glanced back at the cabin. They were going to bed. They'd be sure to laugh at him and tell him to let her take care of herself. But she looked so sick; and it was penetratingly cold.

With a sudden impulse, he ran back to the barn, lighted the lantern and hung it up near the stairway to the loft, and returned to Babsie. The poor dog had started on up the drift, but at sight of him coming back, she lowered herself to the snow again. Kneeling down beside her, Dwight put his hands under her and lifting her from the snow, carried her into the barn and up the stairway to the loft, where he deposited her on a pile of hay. Then he went down again, watered the two horses, closed the barn door, and came up to the loft with the lantern, building himself a cozy fire in the gasoline-drum stove.

Soon the big metal drum was oozing comforting heat. There was the broken portion of an old chair nearby, and on this Dwight sat down so that he could watch Babsie, who lay curled up on the pile of hay.

As soon as she saw him looking at her, she began an effort to wag her tail. She was grateful to him for having brought her up into the cozy loft, he thought; and he was glad he had done so. Babsie was feeling toward him something of what he was feeling for the teacher who had so clearly defended him, taken his part. Dogs had such a simple sure way of showing their gratitude. He wished he might show Miss Martinby how he felt, like that. Words were so hard to find, and when one did find words, they rarely said what one wanted them to say.

The hayloft was a weird-looking place in the orange light of the lantern, hanging on its nail and still swaying slightly. The hay stuffed into the greater portion of it, up to the rafters, reminded him of a picture he had seen once of a python trying to swallow a wild goat. But he loved the big shadows which the lantern threw, loved the warmth of his own stove, and the feeling that he was secluded there, safe from critical eyes and scolding tongues. Here he had had the happiest moments in all the three years he had been with the Burnells; and the best he could have said for the Burnells was that he hadn't been any too happy at the Orphan Asylum in Edmonton.

He was picturing to himself his janitor duties, chopping wood for the teacher and bringing water to the teacher's little house in its corner of the school grounds, when he was startled by a swift patter, and rousing himself, he saw Babsie start down the stairway.

"Here, Babs!" he cried, jumping up.

Only one paw down the first step below the oblong hole in the floor, Babsie stopped obediently, and looked back at him, open mouthed.

"It's much better for y'u up here, Babs," pleaded Dwight, going to her and taking hold of her by the big hairs at the scruff of her neck, pulling her gently back toward the hay. "I'll get y'u some water."

He settled her comfortably back on the hay, and taking his lantern went for the water. Outside of the barn door, he stopped and stared at the log-cabin house, a hundred and fifty feet away. The light poured out of the windows, and smoke shot straight up out of the stovepipe which stuck up from the roof at a slight angle. The stars gleamed with a cold, penetrating brightness in the faraway winter sky. It was a dismally lonely country, so far away from crowded, noisy Edmonton; but never had it seemed so warm with promise as it was this night because the new teacher was in that little house.

He pulled some water up the icy throat of the well and pouring it into a pail that stood nearby, he carried it up to the hayloft. Babsie drank until he began to worry that she was drinking too much, then she wagged her big tail gratefully and curled up on the hay again.

Dwight returned to his dilapidated chair by his fire, and, his cheeks resting on his hands, his elbows on his knees, he half closed his eyes and dreamed. He had been unhappy at the Orphan Asylum, because life had been mechanical in its regularity, going through the routine of the day from one detail to another, always marching in a line of dozens of boys. Here on this little farm, he had been lonely all the time. But now he felt enthusiastically hopeful at the prospect of having Miss Martinby in charge of the school, living in the little teachers' house on the school grounds.

This hope made the old hayloft cozier, and the explosive snaps, as nail heads in the distant corners of the loft protested against the cold, made the kindly fire at his side so much more comforting. And as he sat dozing in its heat, the horses in the barn below stamping their feet restlessly and rhythmically on the floors of their stalls, he fell asleep.

He woke with a start some time afterward, how long he didn't know. The fire had gone out. He was cold and uncomfortable, and the back of his neck was aching so he could hardly turn his head. He rubbed some life into his face, and stumbling toward his bed, was about to sit down on it and remove his boots, when he thought of Babsie. She was not on the nest where he had left her. He stood there, bewildered for a moment. He was tired and sleepy; it would be no pleasure to go looking for her; yet he couldn't go to sleep without knowing where she had gone.

He took down the lantern, and holding it so that he could look around, into the dark places, he called to her. There was no answer. He was about to start down into the barn below, when he heard a small puppy cry, muffled, as if from the other end of the hayloft.

He turned up his lantern wick, as bright as he could make it, and with an upsurge of joy, he pushed his way between the hay and the low wall of the loft till he spied Babsie's tail, in a nest in the side of the hay.

"Babs, you ain't afraid of me," he said, getting down on his knees, and creeping toward her.

When he reached her, Babsie lifted her steaming muzzle to him, appealingly, moving it protectingly over the tiny pup in front of her, even as her big tail flopped up and down placatingly. The pup was sprawled out so that all of his tiny legs were visible. He was a tawny, brownish little fellow, and each of his four legs was white, almost to the knee.

Dwight looked down at mother and baby silently, a strange and gripping awe holding back his desire to chuckle, even though he was so thrilled he could hardly contain himself. Babsie's eyes were bloodshot, and moist as with fever. Cold as it was there, away from the fire, her mouth was open and she was panting for breath. There was no mistaking the fact that she had suffered; yet every cell in her body was burning with a concern for that little thing; and she watched him anxiously, so that he hesitated to take hold of the pup as he wanted to so badly.

"You know I won't hurt it, Babs," he argued, stroking her head affectionately.

Letting his hand gently slip down from her head to the little fellow, he carefully took hold of him. But the tiny little mite clung powerfully to the warm source of his first meal, and he began protesting loudly, as soon as he was torn from it.

"How do y'u know just what to do, y'u little white

paws?" gurgled Dwight, lifting him higher so that he could examine him.

The squirming little fellow beat the air with his white-tipped paws, searching blindly in every direction with his knobby little head. His devoted mother quickly got to her feet, and reaching anxiously for him, licked at him with her hot tongue.

In the midst of this effort to get him back, the little fellow opened his tiny mouth and yawned with all his energy. Dwight studied him, bubbling with joy; then out of sympathy for his worried mother, he lowered him to the hay. Immediately Babsie lay down caressingly around him.

Dwight hastily backed out to the open part of the loft, and rebuilt his fire; then he brought Babsie and her pup out to the nest he had originally made for her, nearer the fire. When she seemed settled and contented there, he took another good look at the pup and very reluctantly went off to bed.

All his sleepiness had gone by this time. What a miracle he had witnessed! Out of nothing, it seemed, a living thing had come, perfectly shaped in every detail, every white-tipped paw, every tiny claw, the little mouth, the little tongue, even the tiny hairs about the delightful little muzzle.

"I'm goin' t' keep 'im!" he cried with such feeling that his voice rang out in the darkness and startled him; and then he added more softly: "He'll just be my own dog. I'll train 'im from the start. He'll do tricks. Wherever I'll go, he'll go with me—always. He'll go to school with me. Just my dog—nobody else's."

Into the very small hours of the night, he lay there planning for his dog, his very own dog—how he would feed him, how he would start his training, how carefully he would guard against anybody else's interfering with his educating him, till his head was in a fever; and then, out of sheer mental exhaustion, he fell asleep.

When he woke again, it was broad daylight; and he was startled to see John Burnell in the loft, standing and looking down at Babsie.

"Did you bring 'er up here?" demanded John Burnell, turning to Dwight.

"Yes, sir," faltered Dwight.

"What'd y'u do *that* for? She's had her nest ready out there in the haystack f'r days."

"She was sick when I came out las' night, an' couldn't climb up the drift."

"When school starts, talk to all the kids, find out who needs a dog, an' give 'em all away, soon's they get a little older."

Dwight had gotten up from under his blankets, and in his stockinged feet had stepped over to Babsie. Burnell's using the word, "all," had made him curious; and he was surprised, when he looked, to see five pups, feeding in a row. He wanted to laugh out with joy, but he was suddenly taken with alarm, as his eye settled on the little fellow with the white-tipped legs; and before he realized what he was doing, he cried out pleadingly: "Can't I keep the little white-paw feller f'r my own?"

"Your own?" cried the farmer, impatiently. "Towser an' Nip an' Babsie *ain't* y'ur own?"

"Not my very own," pleaded Dwight, in that voice which the big farmer said he disliked and which he called "whinin'."

"Jes' get that idea out of your head, fast as y'u can," said Burnell, stepping down the first two steps. "Such a crazy idea! Three dogs t' feed a'ready. There ain't scraps enough t' feed 'em three. Feed scraps t' pigs an' y'u get somethin' back f'r it all."

Dwight's face twisted with worry. He remained standing there, for some time after the farmer had gone, looking down at the pups, too preoccupied to allow himself the pleasure of picking up his little Whitepaw.

His mind raced. He must do something about this terrible situation. Perhaps Miss Martinby might help him out. By the time the pups were old enough to be given away, he would know Miss Martinby better and would be able to ask for her help.

CHAPTER II

The Early Darkness Springs a Leak

CAME a warm spell with a shower of rain. The drops pelted the roof rhythmically. The wafts of wind which occasionally broke into the hayloft became soft and soothing. The hard winter coldness relaxed and the blood which had coursed slowly began to move faster. All things stirred with a new and exciting restlessness.

While the sun shone smilingly, while the stars sparkled through clear, cold nights, while the rain pelted the silver roof of the barn, arched over the secluded world of the hayloft, Whitepaw calmly pursued the mapped-out order of growing into a healthy, fat pup.

That the big farmer wanted him given away or drowned, that Dwight wanted desperately to have him go on living, close to him, that life was a very long trail of adventure, involving pain and hardship as well as pleasure, bothered Whitepaw no more than did the useless tugging and the melancholy whining of the wind around the corners of the barn. The wind which failed to touch him didn't exist, as far as he was concerned. But there were things which in a half-conscious sort of way did begin to interest him, more and more each day.

The overwhelming desire for milk, something to fill up the emptiness inside of him, which came upon him time after time, involving as it did the necessity to rush for a comfortable place to get it, taught him that he was not alone, not the only beneficiary of the good mother who provided it. Repeatedly going through the same process of wanting milk, seeking it, sometimes finding it easily and sometimes having to sit and cry for it, taught him that this mother who was the source of it was not a stationary thing, like the hay or the wall, but a living, crawling-around sort of thing, like himself.

Little by little he became aware of the fact, too, that this mother was not only the source of milk and warmth, but that she loved him, and in a vague way watched over him. Sometimes as he was drawing the satisfying milk, her soothing tongue would reach out and caress him, often driving away some little discomfort which was annoying him.

Life to Whitepaw first asserted itself as a sort of platform or plane of feeling, onto which he occasionally crept, out of the deeps of sleep. When his waking senses, being new and unhardened, wearied of the exertion of being on this plane, he had only to let go his hold of the few small rays of consciousness and slip back into the restful sleep he had come from.

So Whitepaw mainly slept and ate and whined and whimpered when what he wanted wasn't just where he could reach and get it; and then, quite abruptly, the surrounding darkness sprung a leak. The ocean of light, seeping through his newly opened eyes, began flooding the hayloft, giving shape and form to many things; and the sweet contentment of drowsing gave way to a stirring curiosity.

The most important thing which first presented itself to him, in form, upon opening his eyes, was the massiveness of his mother. What he had felt as a comfort-giving foundation of his existence, appeared to be a limited, shaggy-brown creature which stood up and off the solid floor, on tall, thin legs. Near her, and about himself, were the other little creatures who shared her goodness with him.

Often he would sit on his haunches and regard these other small creatures with his bleary little eyes. Sometimes he would lie with his forepaws on one sleepy little fellow, while he gazed at another, a bit farther off, till the gigantic task of studying him became too much for him. He would open his mouth wide, yawn with all his remaining energy, then lower himself on the warm body under him, and drop off to sleep.

But as the hours moved along from day into night, from night into day, and the sleepy periods became narrower, giving way to wider and wider periods of wakefulness, Whitepaw became dissatisfied with merely looking on bleary-eyed at things. As he watched a funny little ear flipping, or a pointed little tail wagging, he would reach out with a white-tipped paw and touch the moving thing. If that effort resulted in nothing in particular, he would reach for it with his mouth. The resistance he would then feel would thrill and challenge him, and drive him to greater effort.

He was not alone in the delight he took in this game of experimenting with the things around him. Often other little mouths seized *his* tail, or *his* leg, or *his* ear; and the manner in which they treated these valuable members of *his* body, taught him the necessary laws which kept the peace in the little family.

This love of experimenting, this love of play became more and more engrossing, until it monopolized every wakeful moment. The more they played, the wider grew the circle of life into which their activities rolled and pommeled them, and Whitepaw began to feel something of the size and the nature of the whole hayloft. The floor, the foundation of everything, separated itself from the walls, from the hay. The hard and immovable things from the soft, movable ones; and from everything, experience soon set Dwight apart.

Dwight grew from a mere odor which was different from all other odors, a color with a peculiar brightness, a touch which, unlike fur, was just as pleasant, into a definite being as important as his mother.

He would sense the strange odor before Dwight would arrive, would feel the approaching tread of boots, and wait with pleasurable expectation to be lifted and cuddled. When he was lifted high into the air, into the warmth which emanated from the big boy's face, he would experience an overpowering urge within himself to lick that face, any part of him within reach, and the muscles of his back and tail and ears would break into blind, unrestrained exertion.

During the long day, when the light came through the dusty window high up in the wall, Whitepaw often awakened to find his mother gone. He would join his brothers and sisters in their wailing complaint against her absence, till he would become tired of doing so, and would move off into the shadows to sniff at and examine the great pile of pungent hay. Moving over the less cluttered spaces around the nest, he always came to the four-inch board which Dwight had set up to keep them from straying.

He would scratch wildly at that board, till his paws became strong enough to lift him up; then he would stand there, holding on to the upper edge, and peer wide-eyed into the fascinating openness beyond. In time the urge to pull himself over the board, so that he might move off without interference into the more promising spaces, became a torment; and he would stand there, *ki-yi-ing* fretfully because he couldn't make it.

Then one day, as he reached and pulled with growing impatience, he suddenly went over, dropping **on**

He would stand there ki-yi-ing *fretfully.*

the other side with a thud and a yelp of fear. At first, Whitepaw was so scared that he made an attempt to get back into the nest; but when, one after another, the rest of the litter came tumbling over the board, his courage returned. He started with considerable caution to explore the surrounding country.

Cowering low to the floor, he made his way around the mountain of hay, constantly turning to look back, to make sure that the others were coming with him. The light out in the open was too bright for him. It kept him afraid, and he crept along carefully, hugging the floor. Suddenly he was startled by the thumping of heavy feet, and he turned so abruptly that he knocked over one of the pups behind him. That little fellow let out a piercing *ki-yi* of fright, and the rest of the litter went scampering back toward the nest.

At the four-inch board they all tried to climb over at the same point, while the heavy, thumping sound came nearer and nearer. Before he managed to get over, Whitepaw felt himself lifted into the air. As he licked Dwight's cheek, against which he was being pressed, Whitepaw became aware of the fact that his mother had also arrived. Dwight was good enough to lower him on the other side of the board; and so Whitepaw's first great adventure ended in a good meal and a long, recuperating sleep.

Since the adventure had ended happily, Whitepaw was very much inclined to repeat it, the next time his mother left them to shift for themselves. But he was disappointed to find that something had happened to the wall which he had climbed before. Another four-inch board had been added to the first. Try as he would, he couldn't even find the edge to pull himself up on. In vain he kept reaching with his paws, only to slip down again at each attempt; and an impatient jump gave him a disagreeable bump on the nose.

That sobered him for a while; but as soon as the sting of it was gone, his curiosity came back stronger than ever. He was not quite so reckless, however, moving along carefully from side to side, over some of his brothers and sisters, who were as busy as he was; and as he got to where the board end was dug into the mass of hay, his nose unexpectedly came upon a spot which gave way as he pushed into it. Before he actually realized what a victory he had scored, he found himself again in the open space of the loft, the rest of the litter again close behind.

Not so much afraid now, Whitepaw's eyes adjusted themselves more quickly to the brighter light; and moving more freely than he had the first time, he soon came upon an amazing variety of things to sniff at, to bite, or to pull.

He came upon an old gunny sack which had held oats. Along with the floury dust which came from it and made him sneeze, it carried a strong scent of Dwight. While the dust bothered him, the scent of Dwight in it interested him. He wriggled affectionately as he sniffed at it, arching his little back and barking, because while it smelled of Dwight, it didn't act like him at all. The other pups imitated him, and their nosing the sack made it move around the floor.

One here and one there, they began biting at it and

trying to pull it away from each other, pulling it all over the open space. Suddenly Whitepaw felt a current of cool air, loaded with strange new smells. Sinking low to the floor, he reached forward with his muzzle and sniffed anxiously at the oblong shadow which lay a few inches away.

As the shadow didn't seem to be moving, Whitepaw soon raised himself to his full height and sniffed harder and harder. Then he began stepping carefully toward it. The nearer he came to it, the stronger did the smells become, and the more penetrating the cold wafts of air. But while his skin was trembling, his curiosity urged him on.

He came to the very edge of the opening in the floor, and was appalled by the manner in which the floor itself dropped away from him. He clung fearfully to the solid edge, his dilated eyes staring wildly at the confusing pattern of lights and shadows on the barn floor way down below him. Yet the more he saw and felt, the more interested he became, moving farther and farther along the edge, to see better. Then his mother appeared, coming swiftly up the stairway, and to his surprise, she snapped at him angrily, cuffing him and pushing him over with her muzzle.

Badly hurt and disappointed, Whitepaw righted himself and pattered away after his brothers and sisters who were already waddling hurriedly back toward the nest. As he beat along after them, he promised himself that he would never go near that opening again. And yet, the very next time his mother left them, he crept back into the open space, going right to the opening in the floor, like a moth into the flame.

For a while, when he went exploring to that opening in the floor, he would keep himself nervously ready to flee back to the nest at the slightest sound; but as time went on and nothing bad came of his going there, the lure of those lights and shadows in the barn below, completely overcame his fears, and he began moving around the opening with perfect ease.

One especially lovely afternoon, when the light poured down from the window with a disturbing, golden warmth, having dragged the gunny sack like a mop over every square inch of the loft space in front of the hay, Whitepaw happened to approach the oblong opening at the end where the stairway came up to meet it, and discovered the first of the steps, directly below him. From where he was, the entire stairway appeared to be one continuous, solid board, leading down to the barn floor.

His eyes glaring at the fascinating lights and shadows, he reached forward a bit too far, to sniff, lost his balance and dropped to the first step. It was not a very great drop, but Whitepaw was so frightened that he didn't even whimper. Merely crouching as low to the step as he could, he hung on for dear life.

When he dared raise his head slightly, to look about him, he was terrified by the feeling that he was on a narrow strip of solidity, almost completely surrounded by abysmal nothingness. Up above him, on the edge of the loft floor, his brothers and sisters were sitting on their haunches in a row, looking down at him sympathetically. He rose to his feet with the impulse to jump back up to them, but the open space between the step he was on and the floor, threatened to engulf him, like an ocean wave, and he quickly shrank back and whimpered.

Merely crouching down to the board of the step, however, wasn't getting him anywhere. As the step continued to be solid all along its length, he crept cautiously toward one end. There, where the side of the stairway reached up to the floor of the loft, he carefully crept up the slant with his forepaws, his hind legs clinging to the first step. Standing that way, he could almost touch the floor with his muzzle; and when his brothers and sisters came running over to him at that end, he made a desperate attempt to jump up to them.

He could hardly have done worse. He not only failed to get up to the floor, but in falling back to the first step, he went off its edge. Down the whole dreadful length of the stairway he rolled, each step rising up as he went and striking him a blow on the back, the head, or the side.

All the way down, he yelped with unrestrained terror; but on the barn floor below, he was so frightened that he instinctively shrank from letting himself be heard. Quickly righting himself, trembling like a grass blade in the wind, he looked about for some covered space into which he could run and hide. Then he felt something approaching him and ran to get under the stairway, but he was suddenly picked up by the scruff of the neck and lifted into the air.

As soon as he felt the affectionate warmth of Dwight's

cheek, his terrors lifted like puffs of bad smoke, and love and gratitude filled him to overflowing. He wriggled his little body, wagged his little tail, and even as he whimpered, very sorry for himself, his hot little tongue licked at everything within reach.

But another voice came roaring out of the confusion; and Whitepaw pricked his ears as he listened for the first time to two human beings, talking to each other.

"When y'u goin' t' start givin' 'em away?" asked the big farmer.

"Mary Lou says she wants 'er pup Sunday," said Dwight, evasively.

"Mary Lou—that's only one—y'u got five of 'em t' give away."

Dwight was about to try another plea for the right to keep Whitepaw, but he hesitated. He was desperately afraid of making a wrong move.

Babsie came along, and seeing that he had one of her pups, jumped upon him, as if to try to take it away. Dwight brushed her down in a sad, preoccupied manner, and then slowly and thoughtfully started up the stairway, while she ran on ahead. The four remaining pups scampered back toward the nest.

In the loft, Dwight put Whitepaw over the two boards with the rest of them; but he stood there in the semidarkness, as if he had lost his memory and didn't know what he had come up for.

CHAPTER III

Stubborn

DWIGHT was up at dawn Sunday morning. He fed and watered all the stock. He milked the cows and separated the cream, while the Burnells were still in bed. He cleaned out all the stalls and bedded them with fresh straw. It was not until he was grooming Billy, the black pony, getting him ready for his trip, that he heard the Burnells stirring about the house and began to smell the breakfast bacon frying.

Dwight hoped that his being so unusually industrious this Sunday morning might put John Burnell in one of his better moods. But when the farmer's voice rang out across the spring morning air, announcing, "Breakfast ready," there was something peculiar in its tone which suddenly shook Dwight's faith in his strategy.

He had thought as he had lain awake, half the night, that his offer would be irresistible. He was willing to get up an hour earlier every morning, from now on—even two hours earlier during the busy summer. He was willing to shoulder all the responsibility of all the chores around the farmyard, so that the farmer himself could give all his time and attention to his crops. He was even willing to hand over to Burnell most of the wages the school board was to pay him for his janitor work. All this he would do if only he were allowed to keep Whitepaw.

Walking slowly toward the log-cabin, he began to imagine the farmer's answers to all his arguments: "Y'u're old enough t' get up earlier now, anyway." "Y'u *should* do all the chores by rights." "I feed'n clothe y'u—you *should* give the janitor money t' me."

Dwight entered the cabin with an effort to look as if there had been nothing unusual in the air, but as soon as he opened the door, he knew that they had been talking about him. He didn't like the smiles that Burnell and his wife were giving each other. They were making fun of his industriousness. They knew why he had gotten up so early and why he had worked so unusually hard.

"What's the matter, Dwight," began Mrs. Burnell at the stove, on the verge of laughing, "what makes y'u so ambitious this morning?"

"Ambitious!" repeated Dwight, flustered and trying to cover up his embarrassment. "I'm goin' t' peddle out the pups, t'day, so I got up early, so's I get the chores done, before I go."

"Sounds too good t'be true," said John Burnell. "What y'u got up y'ur sleeve?"

"Got nothin' up m'sleeve," growled Dwight.

His whole grand scheme had collapsed. How could he even make his offer now?

He went at his breakfast without appetite, slowly deciding, as he ate, to go back to his original plan of asking Ted Mariner to help him out, by taking Towser instead of one of the pups. John Burnell was concerned about having to feed more than three dogs. If Ted took Towser, and he kept Whitepaw, there would still be no more than three dogs to feed. He was worried about whether Ted would want to take an old dog; but Ted was a good-hearted and good-natured old bachelor whom he had always found approachable.

"Y'u got places now f'r all five pups, have y'u?" asked Burnell, abruptly, staring right at Dwight and making him uncomfortable.

"Not all of 'em yet," said Dwight.

"Y'u might go t' see Larry Smith. Larry lost his dog, he told me, when I was t' town t' fetch the teacher. If he ain't got 'im a new dog, he'll be glad t' get a smart pup like that there white-legged one. He might even pay y'u f'r 'im."

Now Dwight was certain that Burnell knew all about his intentions to find a way of keeping Whitepaw; and he realized that the farmer had set himself firmly against it. He knew that arguing would only strengthen Burnell's determination not to give in. Just what he ought to do, he did not know; but he felt that it was best to say nothing for the time being, and so he ate on, in silence.

After breakfast he saddled the black pony, and tied the basket he had prepared for the pups to the saddle-horn. Then, locking Babsie in the oats bin, he brought the five surprised pups down from the hayloft and put them into the basket, covering them up so that they wouldn't be cold, and yet have plenty of air. Finally mounting his pony, he rode away, the pups in the basket answering with tragic wails the muffled barking of their mother in the oats bin.

It was a beautiful spring morning. There was still some snow visible in spots here and there, but by far the bulk of it had melted during the night, and the cool, shimmering water shone in every hollow and indentation, in clear, cool pools, or wide, rippling ponds.

He planned to go to Mary Lou's place first, and give her one of the girl pups, then go on to Ted Mariner's. Burnell rather admired Ted, as a reliable, thrifty man with what he called lots of horse sense; and if Ted should be willing to take Towser, or suggest some better arrangement, it was possible that Burnell might allow himself to be persuaded by Ted.

A mile beyond the edge of the patch of poplar trees which surrounded the Burnell farmyard, Dwight was surprised to see that the slough had filled up completely, covering the road for a hundred yards each way. The lake that had formed was three times as big as it had been Friday, when he had splashed through it on his way home from Faraday's with the mail bag hanging at the saddlehorn. The mail bag had gotten wet. The pups in the basket were not hanging as low, but the pond was deeper now.

He turned across a stubbled field, to the left, but when he reached the top of the hill, and looked down into the Cripps place in the hollow beyond and saw some of the Cripps "kids" running around the yard, he turned still farther westward. If he went through the Cripps yard, the Cripps "kids" would gather about him, hear the pups and ask for one. He wouldn't want a pup of his growing up into a Cripps dog. They were dirty and disorderly people and reputed to be mean to their animals.

As he came to the school road, and turned northward toward the school house, he began to consider seriously the possibility of asking Miss Martinby to keep Whitepaw for him. There was talk in the district of getting Miss Martinby to teach on, up to Christmas, because there had been no school the previous year. By fall, Whitepaw would be a full grown dog. Just how he would manage with Burnell at that time, he didn't know. But at least he would have Whitepaw until that time; and he wasn't going to worry too far ahead. If Miss Martinby were willing to take the pup, he could see him every school day and train him during noon and recess time and during the time after school, while he did his janitor work.

Miss Martinby lived alone in the little teacher's house on the school grounds; and the whole district was talking about how lonely she was. Why wouldn't it make it nicer for her to have a pup; and why wouldn't the whole district, anxious to have Miss Martinby stay on as long as possible, be grateful to him for such an idea?

Dwight urged his pony to a gallop. Soon he came over a knob in the road and saw the schoolhouse, sitting on the flat stretch of prairie a mile away like a toad stool, the little teacher's house in the corner of the fenced-in school grounds so small it looked in the distance like a rock.

As he reached the corner of the barbed wire fence which surrounded the school grounds, Dwight instinc-

tively turned in his saddle to look around. He wanted
to make sure no one was seeing him. There wasn't a
living creature in sight anywhere, though his eyes trav-
eled over miles of flat land in every direction. It was a
lonely place for a young woman to live by herself, even
he could feel that.

The door of the teacher's house was closed and the
place looked as if no one were home, except for the
smoke that was rising out of the funny black stovepipe
which stuck up above the tar-paper covered little
shanty.

Dwight rode through the open gate into the school
grounds and tying the pony to a fence post, he dismounted and let the pups down on the ground. He was
afraid that Miss Martinby might still be asleep or perhaps not quite ready for company, and so he proceeded
to amuse himself with the pups in the schoolyard. He
ran around the schoolhouse, over the little platform
before the door, and laughed to see them struggle up
that little platform as they ran after him.

"Well, Dwight," said Miss Martinby, coming out a
few minutes later, wearing a pretty blue dress with a
very fancy little apron over it, "what brings you here
today?"

"I have t' give the pups away," said Dwight, starting
slowly toward her, the pups at his feet.

"Oh, look at those lovely little fellows," crowed
Miss Martinby, feelingly, crouching down to welcome
them.

At sound of her voice, the pups who had been falling
all over Dwight's feet, stopped and looked up at her,

curiously, interestedly, but not altogether sure of her. At first they backed into Dwight, like chicks pushing themselves against their mother hen; but Miss Martinby's voice, coaxing them, became irresistible, and they began waddling toward her.

"You darling little fellows," cried Miss Martinby, taking hold of one in each hand, raising Whitepaw in her right hand to her cheeks. "Bring them all into the house, Dwight. Let's give them some milk."

Dwight gathered up the other three and the entire litter was deposited on the coyote-skin rug, near Miss Martinby's bed. While Miss Martinby hurried around, getting the pan and warming some milk, Dwight looked about him, surprised at the change Miss Martinby had made in the attractiveness of the little one room house. The last time he had been there was when he had been sent to clean it for her. It had been musty and cold and gloomy that day. Now it was warm and cozy. She had evidently made some candy the night before and the place was smelling strongly of melted sugar and chocolate. The little stove in the corner was red hot. The bed was neatly made up, and the flimsy curtains had been washed and starched. The wall beside the bed was covered with pictures of far away places and people.

When the milk was warmed to the proper degree, Miss Martinby got down on her knees with Dwight, to watch the pups drink it. Over and under each other they greedily pushed their way to the bowl, eager to find the most advantageous position from which to lap, each one concerned about getting all he could get, before the others had it all lapped up, even though there was milk enough there to bloat them all into little balloons. When the bowl had been licked dry, Whitepaw, who had gone clear into it with his forepaws, sat back a few inches and proceeded to salvage whatever milk was clinging to his feet.

"Look it there, look it there," cried Dwight, his face flushed, his eyes shining with delight and enthusiasm, "there's the smartest little feller in the world."

Miss Martinby looked at him and smiled.

"He is beautiful," she said.

Dwight was slightly embarrassed by her penetrating look.

"Gee," he said with an unconscious sigh, "I c'd teach 'im so many tricks!"

"Do you suppose it would help any if I spoke to your father—to Mr. Burnell?"

"Might," said Dwight pensively. " 'N again, it might not. He's liable t' get mad. He says I'm stubborn; but *he's* terrible stubborn. I'm afraid if he says, 'no' t' you, then he'll never give in."

"Would you be happy, Dwight, if I kept him here for you, till I go? I'd really like to have a pup while I'm here. You could see him every day you come to school. On Saturdays and Sundays, too, if you could take a little ride, you could come over and see him—anyway you could always have him again the next Monday."

She laughed as she said this, and Dwight smiled back with embarrassment.

"I'd have 'im t' train all week long."

"Tell your father that I asked you for a pup. Tell him

I said I get awfully lonesome here; and it will really help me a lot to have a little pup around."

"I'll go on now, then, an' give the other pups away," said Dwight, trying to cover up his delight.

"All right," said Miss Martinby. "You'll want to come back and have another look at him, before you go home, so why don't you come back and have dinner with me? Would you like to?"

"Sure," said Dwight clumsily, then, unable to think of the proper things to say to express his gladness, he stooped down and began picking up the four pups.

When at last he had the pups wailing in the basket, trotting away over the flat prairie road, not a soul within earshot, he sang out at the top of his lungs a formless song of pure joy.

Then he sobered down, the pony falling back into a steady fast walk. He felt that a great piece of good fortune had befallen him. Miss Martinby had been nice to him during the first month of school; but he had never felt quite intimate with her, though he secretly worshipped her. He was a little concerned about whether he would behave properly when he was eating with her. He took off his mitten and looked at his hand. He would have to wash. His clothes weren't very elegant. But she must have liked him to ask him for dinner. He had never had such a fine person act so friendly to him. And above all, he would have Whitepaw safe now. In the fall? Well, she would manage Burnell. If not he might even run away, he thought in a vague flash-like thought, seeing himself trudging along the Saskatchewan River to Edmonton where Miss Martinby lived.

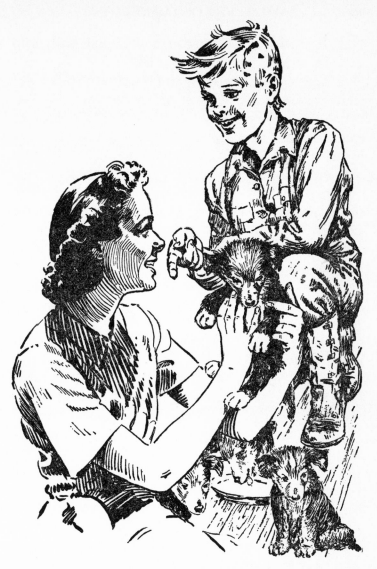

"He is beautiful," Miss Martinby said.

But he dismissed that. All he cared was that now White-paw was definitely his pup, to be trained and managed by him. He would warn the "kids" that they were to keep off. It wasn't good for many people to handle a dog—he knew that.

After trotting and loping across open prairie for three and a half miles and rounding a long drift-lined ridge, Dwight came trotting into the Bingham yard. Little eight-year-old Mary Lou, with flaxen braids hanging down from under her woolen cap, came tearing out of the house. Dwight leaped off the saddle and taking the pup he had set aside for her, he gave it to her.

Mary Lou hungrily seized the pup, and too excited to remember that she ought to thank him for it, hurried into the house. Dwight quickly remounted and rode away before anyone else came out and detained him.

Ted Mariner lived alone in a tiny shanty two miles north of the Binghams, and to save time, Dwight cut across a stubbled field and raced through a small patch of woodland, coming out again into an open space, about a quarter of a mile from Mariner's tar-papered shanty, which stood dismally on a black plowed field.

Ted Mariner was still shaving himself for Sunday when Dwight, a pup in his hand, knocked on his door.

"Hello there, Dwight," he called out amiably, the razor in his hand, half of his beard still covered with lather, "so that's my dog, is it?"

"Yes, sir an' a durn good dog he is, too."

"He is, hey?" asked Ted, returning to his shaving at

the oilcloth-covered table, where the breakfast dishes were still waiting to be washed. "Can he go off by himself an' bring back the cows, for me?"

"Well, shucks!" cried Dwight, who unconsciously talked like the farmers when he talked with them. "Give th' pup a chance t' grow up. Y'u got t' teach 'im."

"Teach 'im?" bellowed Ted. "I'm a busy man; I ain't got time t' be runnin' a dog school."

Dwight's laughter delighted the weather-beaten bachelor. He quickly completed his shaving and leaving the razor soap and water on the table, took the tiny pup from Dwight, and caressed it in his big knotty hands.

"Well, I got t' be goin'," said Dwight, reaching for the door handle.

"Goin'!" cried Ted. "Here I take a dog off y'ur hands, an' y'u ain't even willin' t' stop an' keep me company for a Sunday dinner. That's what I call *in*-gratitood."

Dwight laughed with abandon.

"I got two more pups t' give away."

"Whom y'u givin' 'em to?"

Dwight told him what John Burnell had said about Larry Smith.

"Larry's comin' over here t'night t' skin me in poker."

"Gee," said Dwight. "Suppose I c'd leave one here for 'im?"

"I know he ain't gotten 'imself another dog yet," said Ted, thinking a moment. "Sure, bring the pup in. I'll give it to 'im."

Dwight hurried out and came back with another

pup. The one he had left out in the basket was wailing to high heaven, because it had been left alone.

"Gee, poor thing," said Dwight, lowering the second pup to the floor, nodding in the direction of the door to indicate the pup that was crying itself sick. "I got t' go, Ted."

"Bring 'im in."

"No, I got t' go, Ted."

"What's the matter, y'ur girl waitin' f'r y'u?"

Dwight blushed to his hair.

"Naw! I got t' get back. I have t' find a home for that one yet."

"Where y'u goin' with it?"

"I thought I'd **go** to McBrides—'kids' said they'd want one."

"Why don't y'u go down b' the river here—old Mortimer Jameson, the ferryman, wants a pup."

"He does," cried Dwight, glad to save several miles further journey to McBrides. "I'll go right to 'im now."

So saying he opened the door.

"You don't have to go so soon now, I saved y'u five miles."

But Dwight forged on, Ted Mariner following him.

As Dwight mounted, Ted uncovered the basket and looked in. He seemed to figure rapidly.

"One more," he said, looking sharply up at Dwight. "Where's the white-legged one?"

Dwight looked down at him flustered for a moment. So he too knew all about Whitepaw. Burnell had told him, told everybody.

"Y'u keepin' the white-legged one?" persisted Ted.

"The teacher wanted him," said Dwight, glad that he had not depended on Ted to help him out.

"The teacher!" cried Ted, incredulously. "What'll she be doin' with 'im when she goes?"

The pony was tired of standing there so long, and pulled away. Dwight scolded him loudly for his impatience, but he was glad that his scolding him interfered with his answering Mariner. He wasn't holding the pony back any, and so the pony leaped forward; and hurling his good-by over his shoulder, he galloped away.

By going directly northwest from Ted's place, through the strip of forest which lined the Saskatchewan, Dwight was able to reduce his trip to the ferryman's place by two miles. But he had to pick his way between trees, which still protected deep drifts of snow from the sun.

He came to a path which went down a canyon slope and soon he saw the broad beautiful river. In a clearing on the river shore, he saw Jameson's little log-cabin store, the crooked rusty stovepipe above the rough-shake roof, pouring a river of smoke into the air among the trees.

Right on the shore was the odd-looking ferry raft on which Dwight hoped to ride across the Saskatchewan some day; and old man Mortimer was coming from it when Dwight entered the clearing. The old fellow limped as he came, supporting himself with a stick. When he saw Dwight, he stopped, as if he didn't like to be seen limping. He wore his famous coyote-skin coat, which he had made himself, as well as his much-laughed-over coyote-skin cap with its long point which made him look much taller than he really was.

Dwight tied his pony to a tree, and taking the last of the pups from the basket, started toward the old man, who was still standing in the middle of the clearing, the breeze making his tobacco-stained white beard wag like a dog's tail.

"Ted Mariner said you wanted a good dog, Mr. Jameson," said Dwight, holding up the wailing pup, a faint grin on his face.

"Y'u don't call that a good dog, do y'u?" asked the old fellow, pointing at the pup with his stick.

"It's going to be a good dog," said Dwight.

"And how do y'u know that?"

"I c'n tell by the shape of its tail," said Dwight, knowing how much the old fellow liked to tease. "Mother's the best shepherd dog in the country—half collie."

"How can she be the best shepherd, if she's half collie?"

"The collie in 'er makes 'er a better shepherd."

"Naw Scutch in her, ha' she?" asked the old fellow.

"If there was Scotch in 'er, you wouldn't want the pup."

The old man made a grimace and moved nearer to take the pup.

"You'd be a better mun, if y'u had a bit o' Scutch in y'u."

"Maybe I have," said Dwight, adding more softly, "For all I know."

The old fellow took the pup from Dwight's hands,

and because it was whimpering, he opened his coyote-skin coat and held it partly covered, aginst his body.

"You'll take good care of it, Mr. Jameson, won't y'u?"

"Don't you wur-r-ry about that, lad."

Jameson started off toward the log-cabin store; and Dwight, seeing him go, quietly tripped off to his pony. As he mounted, he saw Jameson turn about, near the door, obviously surprised not to find Dwight beside him.

"Here!" he cried. "Cum here a moment; I want t' show you something."

"I'll come again soon, Mr. Jameson," shouted Dwight, reining his pony about. "I'm late and I have to get back."

Dwight knew that he wouldn't get away for hours, if he didn't go at once. He also knew quite certainly that Jameson had nothing of importance to show him. The old man always desperately tried to inveigle people into his store, so hungry was he for companionship. Dwight had several times before been lured into that store with promises of something he had to show. The last time it was an array of evil-smelling pelts which he was curing, the smell of which multiplied and intensified the stale smells of old groceries and tobacco smoke.

But because he was going back to the delightfully cozy little teacher's house, he was sorry for this poor old codger; and the last glimpse he got of him, standing there helplessly looking after him, the swift waters of the Saskatchewan sweeping by his lonely figure, gave

Dwight somewhat of a guilty conscience. He knew what it meant to be lonely.

Miss Martinby was waiting for him when he trotted up to the schoolyard gate, for it was later than he thought. He had covered a good many miles. She was standing in her doorway and she had little Whitepaw in her hands. As he went through the gate and off to the school barn, Dwight hurried his tying and feeding of the pony, eager to get back to the teacher's house and take the pup into his own hands. And when at last he got into the house and Miss Martinby let the pup down to the floor, the little thing hungrily waddled over to him, running emotionally around and over his feet.

"He's just crazy about you, Dwight," said Miss Martinby, who had gone to take the food from the pots on the stove to serve at the table, turning and looking on. "I believe he's more anxious to see you than he would be to see his mother."

Dwight lifted him and pressed him to his cheek, and Whitepaw wriggled excitedly, licking almost frenziedly at the boy's face.

The table was all set for dinner, and while Dwight washed himself, Whitepaw scampered over his feet, reaching frantically up his legs. When Dwight sat down at the table, Whitepaw lay down on the floor near him with his little muzzle over one shoe. This so touched Dwight that when, without moving his shoe to the slightest degree, he asked Miss Martinby to look, though he was chuckling over it, he was ashamed of a tear that came into his eye. He lifted the little fellow and put him on his lap.

"You mustn't spoil him, Dwight," admonished Miss Martinby, handing him the platter with sliced cold meat. "You know you *can* spoil things by loving them too much."

"That is funny," said Dwight, thoughtfully.

"It is; but it's true, nevertheless."

"Why should it be like that?"

"Well, because children and dogs must learn to live in this world with many people, in many different conditions. If you love them too much and do everything for them, as they want them done, then they get used to having things their own way all the time. As long as they have you around to do things for them, they are all right; but when they get into some condition in which they have to deal with those who won't do things for them, they are lost, are very unhappy."

"I won't always pick him up like that, when I come," said Dwight, apologetically. "I feel kind o' sorry for him t'day, losing his mother an' his brothers and sisters, like that."

"I was only teasing you," said Miss Martinby. "I'm afraid I'll be babying him here, more than you will."

"Do you think it is bad then, t' like kids too well, too?" asked Dwight, his mind still focused on the idea she had expressed.

"Yes, I really do, Dwight. To bring up a child properly, you want to bring him up in such a way that he can take care of himself. Children don't always remain children. They must become men and women who can take care of themselves."

Dwight ate silently a while, embarrassed by the fear that he was not holding his knife and fork properly.

"Ain't it just as bad t' bring 'em up always goin' at 'em, always scoldin' 'em, an'——"

He stopped for lack of words.

"Just as bad," said Miss Martinby, looking right at him; then she went on with a change in her voice: "Dwight, just how did you happen to come out here to the Burnells? Do you mind talking about it?"

"Sometimes I've wanted so bad t' talk t' somebody about it, I could——"

He stopped again, but she said nothing, so that he could continue.

"I didn't like it at the Asylum, in Edmonton," he began again. "I hated it. But Dr. Andrews, he didn't like me much either, he wants t' make a farmer of every boy. I guess he was a farmer himself once. I didn't want to be any farmer, but 'at was a chance t' get away from the institution. I was eleven years old. Mrs. Burnell told me I'd learn t' milk cows an' could have all the cream I wanted. They seemed to want me bad—so I thought it'd be better than the institution."

"That was how long ago, Dwight?"

"That was three years ago."

"Well, did they adopt you?"

"They ain't never said nothin' to me about it," said Dwight shrugging his shoulders. "I don't want t' be adopted by them. I don't want to be a farmer neither. They said if I didn't want to stay on the farm, I could go back. I didn't want t' go back t' the asylum; so I just thought, I'd stay on here till I was eighteen; then I can go where I like. I can, can't I, when I'm eighteen?"

"I really don't know what the law is, Dwight," said Miss Martinby, "but I can find out someday for you. But what bothers me, Dwight, is this: If you don't intend to be a farmer, it seems too bad for you to stay on a farm till you're eighteen——"

"But I don't want to go back to the asylum," said Dwight with an anxiety which made Miss Martinby stop eating and study him. "If I can stay on here till I'm eighteen, I can make my way, I know."

"What would you like to do, I mean when you grow up?"

"I don't know," said Dwight, stopping to think. "Sometimes I think I'd like to be a clerk in a store." He looked at her questioningly, almost embarrassed. "I don't know what I want to be."

"The best thing then, Dwight," said Miss Martinby, "is to get a good education."

"I *want* t' have a good education," he answered. "He says I'll never pass the eighth grade examinations, but ——"

"Let's not even think of what *he* says," Miss Martinby stopped him. "He has his reasons for saying that, but he doesn't really know you, at all. He hasn't given you a chance to show what a fine mind you've got. I'm going to tell him someday what excellent work you are doing for me."

"You'll be goin' away in November," said Dwight wistfully, "an' next year maybe we won't have any teacher; an' then I'll just——"

"I'll send you some books, Dwight; and if you'll write to me, I'll help you from Edmonton. You really have a very good head on you, Dwight, and if you try your very best, there is no telling how far you will be able to go. See what a great man Abraham Lincoln made of himself, all by himself. He didn't have even such books and pencils and paper as you have. I'll send you all the books you need."

"Gee!" said Dwight feelingly, his eyes dilating and reflecting the light. "I'll work so hard!"

He helped her with the dishes, though she said that he didn't have to; and as they worked, she continued to talk of education and books. Never in his life before had anyone told him that he would grow into a fine man. Deeply grateful to her, Dwight now was afire with the determination to prove that she was right.

On reaching home, he found the Burnells around the air-tight heater, as always on a Sunday afternoon, John Burnell reading sleepily out of the Bible and Mrs. Burnell darning socks.

Glad that the farmer was busy, Dwight quietly changed into an older pair of overalls and went out to do his chores. He milked the cows and watered the horses; and when he came back into the cabin, the table, in the lamplight, was set for the usual, makeshift Sunday supper. Even though he was not hungry, having eaten so recently, he ate what he could to avoid the need of making an explanation. In fact, he didn't want to say any more than he had to about anything, and was glad that, for some reason, he was not being questioned.

But when the silent meal was over, John Burnell surprised him by saying abruptly: "I been waitin' t' hear what y'u done with the five pups, but y'u don't seem t' want t' tell about it."

"Nothin' t' tell," replied Dwight. "I gave 'em away."

"All of 'em, Dwight?" asked the farmer, narrowing one eye.

"Sure," said Dwight, his cheeks growing hot.

"Y'u give the white-legged one t' Larry?"

"No, Ted Mariner said he'd take a pup for 'im, an' I left the black an' white an' brown an' white ones."

"Y'u ain't answering my question," said Burnell. "I want t' know what y'u did with the white-legged one."

"I stopped at the schoolhouse," mumbled Dwight, haltingly. "The teacher saw the pups an' *she* wanted the white-legged one."

Dwight, in fear, had been looking down on the floor. Suddenly he felt the floor vibrate with a heavy tread, and felt a hand on his shoulder.

"I knowed all along you was plannin' t' try t' put one over on me," said the farmer, hovering over him. "Y'u made up y'ur stubborn head you was goin' t' keep that white-legged, no matter what I said. So y'u got the teacher t' fix it all up. Well, sir, you'll have t' get up earlier in the mornin' than you do, t' fool me. When the teacher goes, she better take her dog with 'er. There'll be no white-legged dog on this place. First time he shows up on my property, Dwight, I empty my shot-gun on 'im; an' don't you forget that."

So saying, John Burnell took his cap from its nail on the wall, and walked out.

"Don't know why you are always lookin' f'r trouble," said Mrs. Burnell as Dwight dried the dishes she was washing.

Dwight thought it wiser not to answer her. To keep out of the big farmer's way, he went at once to bed, as soon as the dishes were done. But he lay there in mental torment most of the night, wondering what he was going to do when the teacher left for Edmonton, though he never lost hope that she would be able to solve his problem for him, somehow.

When at last he reached the school grounds, early the next morning, and hugging little Whitepaw to him, told Miss Martinby what Burnell had said, she comforted him:

"Well, don't worry about it, Dwight. Do everything he asks you to, and even more. Do your chores well and try to please him. Never mention the pup. I'll talk to him about it, sometime, when he gets over his anger."

"He's awful stubborn," said Dwight.

CHAPTER IV

Loved Too Much

IN SPITE of Miss Martinby's convictions concerning pups and children, and Dwight's philosophically agreeing with her, nobody who saw Whitepaw sitting on his haunches, his two white-tipped forepaws before him pointing like an arrowhead to his knobby, bewhiskered muzzle and the bleary eyes above it, would have been surprised to learn that Whitepaw was loved too much.

For several reasons, Dwight wanted to keep Whitepaw hidden from the rest of the school children as long as possible, but that possibility wasn't very long. Imprisoned in a very comfortable box in the teacher's house, with only the most distant window from the schoolhouse opened for air, Whitepaw's badly spoiled *ki-yi-ing* came pouring into the school yard, shattering the highly desirable silence of the schoolroom. Before the bell rang school into session, at nine, every youngster knew that Dwight had given the now famous, white-legged pup to the teacher; and by the first sound of the recess bell, at ten-thirty, every hungry pair of hands in Miss Martinby's charge had joined the conspiracy to spoil him further.

All through the recess time, eight hilarious youngsters stampeded across the school grounds, while one tiny, tawny pup chased them, mouth open, ears flopping, eyes blazing, and tail wagging.

After recess, Whitepaw had to go back to his box in the teacher's house. Having been led to believe that the world centered around him, Whitepaw thought that all he had to do, to get them to come and take him outdoors again, was to let himself be heard. There was no difficulty hearing him. The great difficulty lay in the efforts of the youngsters not to hear him, not to laugh, not to feel sorry for him. Whitepaw cried till he wore himself out, then, very sorry for himself, he curled up and went to sleep.

At noon, however, when he was taken out again, there was not a trace of resentment on his happy little face. Though he had wailed and *ki-yi-ed* for fully an hour, he romped and wriggled and wagged his little tail as if nothing unpleasant had ever happened to him.

He was allowed in the schoolroom while the youngsters ate their lunches; and he was showered with presents of the most delicate tidbits in each lunch basket, the schoolroom turned into a bedlam of gurgling, laughing, and cooing over him. From every seat, hands reached out to grab him. Everywhere he was lifted and cuddled against warm cheeks; and each time Dwight thundered out his orders to let him alone. But no sooner was he replaced on the floor, than another greedy pair of hands would reach out to take him.

"You'll make 'im sick, handlin' 'im around like that," Dwight argued. "If you kids keep on feedin' 'im things that ain't good for 'im, I won't let 'im come in here noons at all."

Most of the youngsters tried not to offend in that manner, but one of the more aggressive ones challenged Dwight's authority.

"He's the teacher's pup, ain't he?" he shot at him.

"Yeh," Dwight replied, quite flabbergasted at first, "but she told me t' take care of 'im."

All afternoon, Whitepaw tried again to move them with his frantic cries, after he had been returned to his box in the teacher's house, but his frantic cries gradually became just a bit less frantic; and he stopped crying much sooner than he had after the first recess. And when he was allowed to play during the afternoon recess and put back into his box again, he cried for only a few minutes.

But he was happiest when, after school, the children having gone home, he was allowed to run all around the schoolroom as Dwight was busy cleaning it; and he could sniff at everything within his reach. While Dwight washed the blackboards, he busied himself at each desk, recalling the different youngsters by the scent each had left there of himself.

A good deal of his enthusiasm for sniffing at things came from the vague hunger in his puppy soul for his mother and his sisters and brothers, a vague puppy hope that as he sniffed the various things in his reach, he might suddenly come upon them. But that anxious sniffing, like the "why's" of a little child, taught him a great deal about this new world into which he had come.

The old organ in the corner smelled of mice, as had some of the nooks and corners in the hayloft. The wood in the vestibule smelled of other things which he remembered sniffing elsewhere. The chalk dust under the blackboards gave out a new smell altogether. And all these different smells he stored away in his little mind, as children store away words which they learn to know and to spell.

Having sniffed at everything within reach, he began straining to reach things that were way up above the floor. When he could do nothing else, he seized things with his mouth and pulled at them. At soft things, like rags, because they gave when he pulled, he would growl as he pulled and shake his head triumphantly and ferociously.

Pulling at a rag, under the chalk box, the thing came crashing down to the floor near the teacher's desk. He was badly frightened, and backed away as Dwight rushed to him. And when Dwight scolded him as he picked up the many pieces, Whitepaw got the feeling that this was something he shouldn't have done. But since nothing more disagreeable than scolding resulted, he reached cautiously toward the mess on the floor and sniffed. He didn't particularly like the smell of chalk, but that was the smell about which he had been curious from the first time he had come into that schoolroom. And that was the smell which settled itself down in his mind like a word *for* the schoolroom.

Then, as the puppy reached for one of the white pieces of chalk, Dwight picked him up and hugged and caressed him, till it almost hurt him. But he wriggled his little body happily for he knew that Dwight loved him, and Dwight's love filled up the deep-seated emptiness which was his hunger for his mother and his brothers and sisters.

Dwight went back to his cleaning, bringing in a pail with soap and water, and every move Dwight made, Whitepaw followed him. Everything Dwight used, Whitepaw had to sniff at or bite into. When Dwight splotched soap and water on the floor with his mop, Whitepaw plunged right into the puddle, going down on his side and making a mess of himself, but remaining nonetheless curious, if uncomfortably wet. And Dwight spent half an hour trying to keep him wrapped up in an old sweater under the stove to dry, without any great success.

When he had to take Whitepaw into the teacher's house and leave him there and go home, Dwight felt so bad he could hardly say good night to Miss Martinby. And next morning he arrived half an hour earlier than necessary, eager to see the waddling little fellow.

In this reluctant leaving of the school grounds each late afternoon, and in this coming early and breathlessly eager, each morning, time went very swiftly for Dwight. And time went swiftly for Whitepaw, too. In his rapid growth and development, Whitepaw loved every youngster in the school, each taking his place in his mind in some other sense or scent. So regular did his life become, in the weeks that followed, that he began to understand something of the difference between Saturday and Sunday, and the rest of the week.

The days grew warmer and warmer. Well-fed, well-exercised and very happy, Whitepaw grew with unbelievable rapidity, until he began to look like a full-grown dog, reddish-brown all over with white legs and a rich white breast, a more pointed muzzle and a big, bushy tail.

They began to leave him outdoors during class time, merely shutting the schoolhouse door to him. The first day, hearing the youngsters inside reciting in strange rhythmic droning, curious to find out what it was all about, he scratched at the door and whined, till Dwight came out and scolded him. After that he waited patiently until the youngsters broke out of the schoolhouse of their own accord.

He learned that between recess periods and the noon hour, he must entertain himself and be quiet, and when he got tired of sniffing around without the children, he would curl up on the door step and snooze, half listening to their recitations, till the bell would ring. Then he would leap up with joy upon the first one who came out.

If he happened to be particularly energetic, when it was necessary to wait outside by himself, he would wander down to the barn and sniff at the heels of the horses standing there. Each horse would turn his head and look back at him concernedly a moment, then go on with his chewing hay, or just stand and doze.

When he had become thoroughly acquainted with everything on the school grounds, he began strolling off during the long school sessions, into the open fields, beyond the school fence. Up on some round little knoll, he would sit on his haunches and look off into space and sniff the summer breezes, till he would spy some living thing, stirring about. If he saw a little gopher, he would race toward him enthusiastically. The gopher, of course, uttering a shrill whistle of fright would scamper to his hole, and flash out of sight. Whitepaw would trot up to the hole disappointed and, sniffing the gopher, would try to dig down to him. Sometimes he would dig frantically till the school bell would ring, when he would abandon his digging and go tearing back to the shouting youngsters, the strain of loping on his happy face like a laugh.

Joining the children, every one of whom took the trouble to greet him, calling him and petting him, he would wag his tail with all his strength and wriggle his whole big body. Then leaping at this one or that one, he would go running and jumping wildly over the yard, barking for sheer happiness.

However kindly Whitepaw felt toward each child that came to the school, he belonged heart and soul to Dwight. Some of the boys envied Dwight and insisted that Whitepaw liked them as much. And when Dwight bragged of his devotion, some of the boys challenged him.

Billy Farady, the biggest of the boys next to Dwight, brought his lunch basket out one recess time, and giving Whitepaw a piece of a cooky, challenged Dwight to walk off up the road calling him, while he fed him. Whitepaw accepted the pieces of cooky, greedily; but the moment he saw Dwight walking away, he became visibly nervous. As soon as Dwight called, he turned from the cooky offered him and darting under the fence, went galloping after him.

Still unconvinced, Billy—who liked Whitepaw and

whom Whitepaw showed evidence of liking—insisted on making the test in reverse. Dwight was given cookies to feed Whitepaw, while Billy walked off and called to him. Upon hearing his name, Whitepaw pricked his ears and looked after the boy, even starting in his direction a few steps; but appearing nervous and uncertain, he nevertheless remained right with Dwight.

Whitepaw belonged heart and soul to Dwight.

When the bell rang them all back into the classroom, Billy grudgingly admitted defeat. After that, no one questioned Dwight's superior place in Whitepaw's affections.

The love that was so evident between them appeared to have established a special line of communication between them, so that Whitepaw seemed to know at once what Dwight wanted of him. In a very short time,

Dwight had taught him all the tricks known in dogdom. He taught him to speak softly or loudly, to sit up and to roll over, to play hide-and-go-seek with the children, and to make a bow.

His ability to bow proved to be his most profitable trick. The youngsters would be thrown into uproarious delight on seeing this performance, and would give him the best morsels from their lunch baskets to get him to repeat it. Repeating the trick so often, Whitepaw became perfectly expert in doing it. He would stretch out his forepaws, arching his back, lower his muzzle till it touched his paws, then spring back with his mouth open, as if to join the laughter which invariably broke out.

Just as Dwight tried harder each day to teach Whitepaw some new trick, because the other boys and girls delighted in his performances, so Whitepaw seemed to try harder to learn, because he enjoyed the applause he got. When his audience responded to a trick with noise and laughter and showered him with caresses and things to eat, his eyes radiated with satisfaction and pride, and his tongue would loll out of his mouth for joy and excitement.

The more Whitepaw learned, the wiser he showed himself to be, the greater were the privileges granted him. When a bad thunderstorm came along, the pupils were as concerned about his being out in the rain as if he had been one of them. While the lightning flashed and the thunder peals shook the little schoolhouse, they pleaded till they had persuaded Miss Martinby to let him come into the schoolroom, during the school session.

He came in most gratefully, his big eyes looking up as
if he were very sorry for himself, his great fur coat wet
to the skin. Dwight ordered him to lie down near the
stove where he could dry out. And because he lay there
quietly, and because the pupils made no fuss over his
being there, he was allowed to come into the schoolroom next day, even though it was not raining. After
that, as soon as the bell rang, Whitepaw would slink up
to Dwight's heels, and file into the schoolroom, as if he
were one of the pupils.

For some time, Whitepaw would lie down right by
the stove, where, as the various classes went to the front
to recite, he would watch them, trying to make out
what their rhythmic rattling might mean. He would
turn and twist his head so amusingly that the youngsters
were forced to giggle with their hands over their
mouths.

Afraid that this would lead Miss Martinby to prohibit
his coming into the schoolroom during class time,
Dwight taught Whitepaw to lie down under his desk;
and so Whitepaw learned to take his place under
Dwight's seat, as soon as he entered.

At the end of that happy summer, Whitepaw came
to his full size, as big as a calf, his tawny hair sleek and
rich with a dark tingle, his breast white and fluffy, his
slender legs remarkably white-tipped, his great, under-
standing, lively eyes radiant with the love he bore everybody, well-mannered, well-behaved, with a sense of
humor as evident as the good-will that glowed all over
him.

From Miss Martinby's arising in the morning to the

time when she extinguished the kerosene lamp at night, Whitepaw knew every step in the routine of the day. After breakfast, as soon as they heard the hoof-beats of Dwight's pony coming along the hard road, Miss Martinby would open the door for him and let him out. Leaping up in a frenzied desire to touch Dwight's legs in the stirrup, Whitepaw would run excitedly from one side of the pony to the other, in front of him; and then, while Dwight dismounted, he would try as frenziedly to jump up and lick his face. When Dwight had tied his pony in his stall in the school barn, he would turn upon Whitepaw, stroke him and pet him and pommel him, rolling him over on the ground.

In the schoolhouse, Dwight would hang up his coat and hat and proceed to build a fire, on frosty mornings when a fire was necessary. Getting an armful of wood in the vestibule, he would patiently teach Whitepaw to carry one stick to the stove. His tail up with pride, his eyes glowing with satisfaction, Whitepaw would pull or drag the stick to Dwight's side at the stove and quickly turn and go for another.

When the pupils began coming, he always liked to be outdoors to greet them, welcoming each as if his doing so were a necessary part of the school routine.

The recesses and the noon hour were the most exciting periods of each day. And the hour or so that Dwight cleaned the schoolhouse or the barn, or chopped wood, after the youngsters had gone, was always a time of richest devotion between them, saddened subtly by the feeling that the day was ending and the time was approaching for Dwight to leave. When Dwight began stroking him and talking to him in that low voice which Whitepaw had come to understand meant that he was going, he would lower his head and wag his tail slowly and sadly.

Dwight would then take hold of him by the long hairs at the scruff of his neck and lead him into the teacher's house and close the door upon him. Whitepaw would stand near that door, inside, his muzzle tight against the crack, until he heard Dwight come out of the barn with his pony, until the rapid tattoo of hoof-beats had broken upon the stillness and had died away down the road. Then he would go to his special spot near the stove and lie down with a sigh.

The dusk would deepen into night. The firelight, breaking through the cracks in the stove, would swell out into a comforting glow. The lamp would be lighted on the table. Delicious smells of cooking would fill the air. The teacher would load up his dish, and she herself would sit down at the table. Often she talked to White-paw as she ate, and always that made him feel better.

After dinner, Miss Martinby would bustle about with the dishes and her house-cleaning; then she would put on strange tortoise-shell glasses and sit down to read. Feeling lonesome, Whitepaw would move closer to her, and sometimes he would lay his muzzle on her foot.

While she sat there reading quietly, Whitepaw would doze and dream, living over again the most exciting ex-periences of the day. Often, when he recalled some especially affectionate thing Dwight had done that day, he would imagine he heard his voice. He would wag his tail vigorously or sit up, startled. The teacher would turn from her book and looking down at him through the space between her glasses and her cheeks, would ask:

"What's the matter, Whitepaw? You dreaming?"

Whitepaw would look up at her, pound the floor with his big tail as he wagged it, then slip back to his dreaming.

In this happy manner, the summer rolled by. And the cool, autumn winds, coming out of the gloomy, clouded northern skies, brought a disturbing sense of change into the air of the prairie.

CHAPTER V

Very Strange Doings

THERE came that uncertain time, after the end of the summer, when the skies seem unable to rid themselves of the dark clouds which ooze up from beyond the northern horizon; when the winds go tearing down the roads, ripping the leaves from the trees and sending the dead thistles rolling away over the prairie.

The children came to the schoolhouse wearing heavier clothes; and, disliking the constant tugging of the wind, began spending most of their play time sitting around the big stove in the center of the schoolroom. When they played their games, they sometimes managed to give Whitepaw some part, and every move he would make, trying to do what they asked him to, would make the room rattle with their laughter.

On rainy days, Whitepaw would lie near the stove, his wet fur steaming in the heat, listening to the patter of drops on the roof which would accompany the droning recitations, or the ticking of the clock on the wall. And when the shorter days started darkening rapidly, and the pupils, including Dwight, left the school grounds to a wintry quietness, Whitepaw would merely transfer himself from the school stove to the stove in the teacher's house.

The rains which kept coming, one after another, gave

way to a cold, penetrating dryness in the air, in which the sun, when it shone, was brassy and without heat. The mornings came bleak and gray upon an earth which was white with frost, and the frosty whiteness stayed on longer and longer as the days rolled on toward winter.

An early snow came fluttering out of the skies. To Whitepaw it was a new experience, yet the snow was so much like the frost he had been finding every morning, that it didn't worry him. Not being concerned with why things happened, he accepted it in a few minutes, as if he had lived through many winters. When the boys threw snowballs at him, he tried to catch them, as he had learned to catch pieces of food thrown at him. And when they hurled the snowballs at each other, he would race after them, churning the snow into clouds of dust as he ran, leaping high into the air to get at them, and barking as if he had gone crazy.

When the snow melted away again, leaving the barren earth hard and dry, he would stand still for several minutes at a time, the wind tugging at his long, winter hair, and look away over space to the murky horizon, wondering where it had gone, hoping to see the flakes come fluttering down again.

Came a Friday afternoon with strange doings. From the start there had hung in the air a sense of suppressed excitement, and over the teacher and her pupils an unmistakable gloom. Instead of playing the usual noisy games before school assembled, though it happened to be quite nice outdoors, the children stood around the teacher's desk, talking with an unnatural restraint.

When the bell rang at nine, Whitepaw took his place beside the stove. But he sat there with head erect and ears pricked, puzzled by the noticeable brightness about each of the youngsters and even about the teacher herself, his muzzle working rapidly, as he tried to find the meaning of the change that had come over them.

And even more surprising, the noon hour was spent in the teacher's little house, where a table had been fixed up, so large that he had to push his way under it, for it took up all the room there was. The children sat around the table, eating; and so busy were they, that they hardly noticed him at all. Dwight, however, against whose leg he crouched, kept giving him pieces of food every few minutes, always caressing him with his hands when he did so.

After this strange meal, they didn't go out to play, nor did they go back into the school house, though it was still broad daylight. Instead, they went off to the barn to get their horses, one by one, each one stopping to pet Whitepaw, in a way which made him feel bad. Then abruptly mounting their horses, they rode away.

Dwight went into the teacher's house and helped the teacher do away with the big table and set things back into place. Yet, when they ceased working and sat down to talk, things did not seem to be the same as they had been. A subtle change had come even into their voices, as they talked.

"Don't worry about it, Dwight," said Miss Martinby. "He is going to drive me into Vermillion. It will take about two hours to drive over the thirty-seven miles.

That will give me time enough to convince him that I really wanted the dog.

"I'm going to tell him that you have done more than two years schoolwork in these last ten months, that you have real ability and will make a fine man. I'm going to make him realize that someday he will be proud of you. Just leave it to me, Dwight. I'll make him feel ashamed to keep you from the one pleasure you *can* have here. He'll let you keep Whitepaw, I'm sure.

"About your studies, I will get you the books you should have. You study hard, all winter, and next spring, even if you should have no school here, you can go into town and take the eighth grade examinations there. I'm sure you could pass them even now."

Whitepaw was watching the teacher, as she turned her face toward Dwight, when he suddenly heard the distant rattle of John Burnell's old flivver. Whitepaw gave a snappy bark and rushed to the door. Dwight quickly opened it and ran toward the barn, calling to Whitepaw as he ran. Whitepaw wanted to stop in the middle of the yard and look off into the direction from which the car was rumbling, but Dwight shouted at him to follow, and tearing into the barn, quickly shut the door.

This was very strange behavior to Whitepaw, but since Dwight remained in the barn with him, he wasn't concerned about it. Dwight stopped against the crack in the door and peered out. Disliking the dark coldness of the barn, Whitepaw sat down on his haunches so that he could feel the leg of the boy against his side and waited patiently.

Whitepaw heard the automobile start up again, and soon its rattle moved off down the road. Dwight opened the door slowly, and they stepped out into the yard. For a few minutes Dwight stood there quietly looking after the automobile, then he walked back into the barn and brought out his black pony, tying him to the gatepost. When Dwight again walked into the barn, Whitepaw innocently followed him. Inside the barn Dwight began caressing him, stroking his head and talking to him as if he wanted him to do something. Suddenly, however, Dwight stood up straight and turned to leave the barn, and when Whitepaw tried to follow him out, Dwight pushed him back and shut the barn door upon him.

Whitepaw was unhappy and much disappointed, although he felt that Dwight would never do anything mean to him. He sat down on his haunches near the crack in the door and sniffed the cool stream of air which came through it, uncomfortable and worried, yet having faith that Dwight would be coming back to release him.

When he heard the sound of hoof-beats and realized that Dwight had gone off and left him there, he was bewildered. From one end of the barn to the other he raced nervously, leaping up futilely toward the windows beyond the mangers, and running breathlessly back to the door.

Dwight rode away, his mind in a turmoil. What with Whitepaw's unhappiness, imprisoned in the cold barn, he was now not at all sure of Miss Martinby's ability to change John Burnell's mind about allowing him on the farm. By the time he reached the Burnell farmyard, he was convinced it would be best for him to have his chores done well and early. He changed his clothes at once and went to work, cleaning the stable thoroughly, bedding all the stalls, milking the cows, chopping some wood, and watering the stock.

He was sitting near the air-tight heater, waiting anxiously for the farmer's return, when the familiar rattle drew, at last, into the yard. Dwight could hardly endure the pounding of his heart, when the door opened and the farmer came in with a big box of groceries in his arms.

When they sat down to the table for supper, John Burnell ranted against the Vermillion grocers because they charged so much for everything. Since he didn't even mention Miss Martinby or the dog, Dwight began to feel that the teacher had succeeded in persuading the farmer to let Whitepaw come to the farm, that he was avoiding the subject because he hesitated to admit that he had changed his mind.

The suspense tormented Dwight, however. Suppose the farmer went on talking like that for hours? It was getting late, and Dwight feared that Whitepaw might die of grief, imprisoned in that disagreeable barn all night.

The farmer leisurely finished his meal, then abruptly turning to Dwight, he said bitterly: "Well, y'u thought y'u had it all fixed up—the teacher arguing me int' lettin' y'u have y'ur way, didn't y'u?"

Dwight looked up pleadingly. What could he say?

"I told y'u reasonable enough, long time ago. We got three dogs a'ready. It costs money t' feed a pack o' dogs.

"Well, y'u thought y'u had it all fixed up!"

It's downright crazy t' have more'n three dogs on a farm. I said, 'Dwight, the pups have got t' be give away —*all* of 'em.' What'd you do? You thought you could put one over on me. The teacher wants the white-legged one. Keep him the ten months o' school for y'u. Grows up t' be a big dog then, John Burnell, he'll be fool enough t' let y'u have y'ur way.

"You're just a stubborn kid, Dwight. I never heard of such a stubborn trick in all my life; an' if you go on bein' that stubborn, there'll be no livin' with y'u.

"I just said nothin' to her. She went on chatterin' all the way to Vermillion—never shut her mouth a minute. I never let her know a thing—said nothin' to 'er about it at all. 'T weren't none of her business at all. She was hired t' teach kids t' obey their parents, not t' disobey them. I just said to myself, 'He's got t' have the lesson of his life right now, or there'll be no livin' with 'im.' You got yourself into this mess; it's up to you, Dwight, to get out of it. Only remember what I told you. The first time that dog comes on my place, I'll give 'im the shot gun."

Dwight sat up, his pale lips pressed together, his eyes blazing. He had been worrying for weeks about what life was going to be like with school closed and Miss Martinby gone. If at least he could have Whitepaw with him! As it was, this was worse than the orphan asylum. This exacting man and his glum wife, the log-cabin home, the lonely remote farmyard—the place suddenly became unendurable to him. Like Whitepaw in the school barn, he was imprisoned. He must find a way of getting to Whitepaw, of getting away——.

The farmer seemed to divine some of the dark thoughts which blazed out of his eyes.

"An' if you don't like the laws of this home," he said, "y'u better go get y'urself another one. I'll not have a kid in this house who disobeys me an' is stubborn like a mule."

Dwight got up and went behind the curtains, sitting down on his bed to think. He wouldn't give up White-paw, that was certain. If he could get to Edmonton, Miss Martinby would help him. She believed that he had a good head and would make an educated man. Just what that meant he wasn't quite sure; but he believed it was far better than working on this farm for his bread and butter and a pair of new overalls, once a year.

Going to Edmonton on foot would be a great ordeal, but if he had courage, was not afraid, he could make it in four or five days.

As he sat there trying to make up his mind, he heard Mrs. Burnell say, "Why do y'u want t' drive the boy away, like that?"

"I'm not drivin' 'im away," Burnell answered, without attempting to lower his voice. "I said if he didn't like this home, t' go an' get himself another one; an' so he can, by gosh."

"He'll get it into his head t' run away," Dwight heard her whisper.

"Let 'im go!" said Burnell. Then Dwight heard him add in a lowered voice, "Don't worry; he ain't in no hurry t' go."

"I *am* going!" cried Dwight, encouraged by the

vague picture of a glorious future in which he would be changed by study and opportunity into a fine man. "I'm going right now."

"Go ahead!" cried Burnell, his voice belying the arrogance of his words. "I ain't fallin' on y'ur neck, beggin' y'u t' stay."

"I'm takin' m' rifle an' m' clothes," said Dwight. "I worked for 'em."

"Y'u ain't overworked y'urself, but go ahead. Better take a couple o' blankets, too. Y'u'll need 'em, sleepin' outdoors."

"All right," said Dwight, trembling slightly with the thought. "When I get t' Edmonton, I'll send 'em back."

The farmer walked off to his bed. Dwight lighted his lamp and looked about for his belongings. This was an awful thing he was undertaking, but there was no alternative. Certainly he wouldn't give Whitepaw away. He took his twenty-two rifle from the corner and loaded the magazine; then he put the rest of the cartridges into his pocket.

Quickly gathering up another shirt, two pairs of socks, some underwear, and two handkerchiefs, he folded these into his blankets and rolled them up. Then he put on his heavy sheepskin coat, threw the roll of blankets around his neck, put on his cap, and taking his gun, started out.

The old lady was waiting for him near the stove.

"Don't be foolish, Dwight," she whispered. "He don't mean for you to really go."

"Come back soon's y'u're ready t' show some sense," shouted the farmer from his bed. "We'll find a good home f'r the dog. Y'u can't have that dog an' stay here. It's your will against mine, an' I'm boss in my house."

Dwight opened the door and plunged out into the descending night, afraid to say goodbye, lest opening his mouth would betray the fears that were gathering like a storm in his mind.

Once he had broken from that doorway, he wanted to get away before the farmer could order him back. He *was* afraid, but now anything that might befall him was better than going back.

The three Burnell dogs escorted him to the gateway, leaping upon him as he hurried along, but Dwight ordered them to go back. Refastening the barbed wire gate nervously, he lunged forward at so fast a walk, he was almost running.

Somehow, after he had raced along for half a mile, a hidden courage within him asserted itself. He had nothing to fear. He would have Whitepaw with him. He had his gun and could protect himself; he could shoot well; and he had roasted wild prairie chickens over an open fire with Ted Mariner. Young farmers in the district often went to work in Edmonton, during the winter months, and he had heard several say that they preferred to go along the shores of the Saskatchewan. To take the road, he would have to walk thirty-seven miles to Vermillion before he could reach the main highway to Edmonton; and he would have to go by the farmyards of most of the people of the district.

When at last Dwight got to the barn in the school yard, Whitepaw was so frantic he couldn't quiet him down. He barked loudly and whined complainingly and ran around the yard as if he had gone crazy.

Dwight carefully reshut the school barn door, then made his way to the schoolhouse. In the schoolroom, he felt his way to the teacher's desk where he had deposited the key to the teacher's house that afternoon, and found it without even striking a match.

On his way to the teacher's house, he stopped a moment and stared into space. A beautiful clear sky arched over the prairie night, and millions of stars blinked smilingly in it. Though the schoolhouse stood on an open stretch of prairie, so sparse were the settlements there, that no house light was visible anywhere in the night.

Inside the teacher's house, Dwight carefully hung one of his blankets over each of the two windows, before he lighted the lamp; then he proceeded to build himself a fire. Soon the warmth was pouring out of the stove, and with a sigh of relief, Whitepaw lay down in his accustomed place near it. As he lay there, he watched Dwight anxiously through the sides of his eyes.

On the table stood the large tin box into which Dwight had helped Miss Martinby pack the sandwiches which had been left over from the farewell party, at noon. On one side of the tin box, stood a paper one, into which Miss Martinby had placed a whole cake, one that hadn't been touched, and on the other side was a large grocery bag, almost filled with cookies.

Dwight recalled Miss Martinby's saying that it was wrong to throw away good food, but no one had wanted to take any home. Someone had said that there was to be a dance at the schoolhouse, Saturday night, and Miss Martinby had decided to leave everything for the dancers who were sure to be having a midnight supper.

"If they have a dance," thought Dwight, gloating over his good luck, "they'll prob'ly bring more stuff'n they c'n eat, anyway. I'm going to take all this with me."

He fed several of the sandwiches and two of the cookies to Whitepaw for his supper, then he put out the light, took down the blankets from the windows and went to sleep on the bare mattress.

Dwight was up again before dawn. He ate a sandwich for his breakfast and gave one to Whitepaw. Unwilling to take time to build a fire, he quickly packed up his food, rolled up his blankets, and straightened things in the house. He replaced the key in the teacher's desk in the schoolroom, and headed across the fields toward the river, while it was still dark.

The early morning sky was more brilliant with stars than the night sky had been. The earth, everywhere, was white with frost, and the cold silence, now that a new day was coming, gave him a sense of safety.

But Dwight walked fast to get to the clump of trees in the distance, so that he could plunge into the cover of their shadows. Now that he had made the break, he wanted nothing to hold him back. For all he knew, John Burnell, suspecting that he would spend the night in the teacher's house, might be on his way to make him go home with him.

"Even if he *let* me take Whitepaw home with me, I

wouldn't go back now," he cried, as he slipped like a coyote into the strip of darkened woods.

By the time he reached the rim of the river's canyon, daylight showed itself cold and bright-gray above the distant treetops.

CHAPTER VI

"Y'u Got t' Fight for Y'urself"

THE dead grass on the slopes of the canyon, the weeds and bushes along the shore all covered white with frost, the trees standing everywhere in the soft light of early morning, motionless and silent, the river surface moving along peacefully, reflecting the dawn light in the sky— there seemed no reason, to Dwight, to be afraid.

When he had gone beyond the Vermillion district, where people would not know of the Burnells, if the river shore should prove difficult, he might go up to the rim of the canyon and find a road along the prairie, where at some farmhouse now and then, he might get a meal and a night's sleep. He would tell people that he was on his way to Edmonton to find work, and that was true. There would be nothing unusual about that; and where people did not know of Burnell, they would not be suspicious of him.

He had never really been happy at the Burnells, having hung on only because he had been afraid to complain or even more afraid to make any kind of change. Now that he had broken away, nothing could induce him ever to go back. Miss Martinby would help him find work. He was willing to work hard, and in the city hard work would be rewarded.

Whitepaw was beside himself for excitement. The

broad, swift river, glowing in the still faint light, the trees and the rocks all flooded with deep shadows, were strange to him; but Dwight was there with him, and with Dwight nothing worried him. There was in this unexpected freedom to leave the school grounds with Dwight, coupled with the strange doings of the day before, a subtle promise of adventure.

The sun soon appeared over the treetops behind them. It began growing warmer and more pleasant. The colorful, fragrant air made walking a pleasure; and the constantly changing scenery was full of unending interest.

The canyon walls, high and rocky for a space, fell away into a deep, tree-filled hollow. The thick forest, packed with shadow, began thinning out, ending in a swath of grassy, level glade which stretched away like a broad avenue through the woodland strip which lined the river. Then the trees reappeared, as they trudged along, and the canyon walls gradually lifted up again, sheer and steep, and cluttered with boulders and windfalls and bluffs which sometimes jutted right over the frozen shore line.

But the Saskatchewan with its icy fringe went on without end, the soft gurgle of water beyond the edge of the ice intensifying the stillness of the desolate, uninhabited country surrounding it.

Birds appeared from time to time above the treetops in front of them, but they came upon no living creatures until sometime in the afternoon. Whitepaw, so thoroughly at home in that wilderness by this time that he often ran on ahead of Dwight, saw before him, as they began rounding a curve in the river bed, a small group of cattle.

At first he slowed down a bit, worried by the way in which they were gathering together in a bunch, all looking toward him. He continued slowing down till Dwight came to within a few feet of him. As soon as Dwight saw the cattle, he raised his hand, and pointing with his rifle at the bull who was now bellowing and pawing the ground, he shouted: "Sick'm, Whitepaw!"

It was clear to Whitepaw that Dwight wanted him to go on toward the bull, and so he sprang recklessly forward. But when the huge bull lowered his head and flourished his ugly, pointed horns, Whitepaw was filled with doubt. Glancing back toward Dwight a moment, he lowered himself to the ground, wriggling his body and wagging his big tail.

The bull was in no playful mood. Moving down upon him cautiously, one large round eye on Dwight, he struck at the dog with one horn. Whitepaw leaped out of reach, but crouched down again, lifting a foreleg in a friendly gesture, exposing his soft white breast.

At that moment, just as the bull was about to crush the life out of him with a hoof, a stone came flying through the air, hitting him square on his curly-haired forehead. An angry bellow came out of the bull, but he turned and started up the canyon slope, the cows already racing on ahead of him.

Whitepaw thought this was great fun and started racing after them, but Dwight who had dropped his blankets and bundles to the ground, called to him angrily, while he was stooping to pick them up again.

"Y'u're too durn good," Dwight shouted at him with an anger which Whitepaw could hardly endure. "He'd 'a' killed y'u, y'u foolish pup! Y'u got t' fight for y'urself! Everybody ain't goin' t' be kind to y'u like the kids at school."

Whitepaw wagged his tail feebly, looking up at him through the sides of his eyes, hoping to see him smile again. But Dwight continued scolding, even after he had started plodding on, and Whitepaw followed forlornly at his heels.

They came to a windfall in their way, from which the sun had eaten away all the white frost; and Dwight dropped his blankets and bundles on it and sat down to rest. After a little while he got up, and walking to the river shore, went out upon the ice. With a stone, he broke a hole in the ice, and stretching out on his stomach, began to drink.

Whitepaw, who had followed him, stopped beside him and looked on. Five or six feet ahead, he saw the darker water moving along, and he decided he'd trip out there and sniff at it. But before he got near enough to sniff, he began to feel the ice under him lowering itself away from his feet, and a wave of freezing water swept over his paws. He heard a yell from Dwight, and turning anxiously toward him, he went down on his side in water which was now five or six inches above the ice.

Dwight whistled and shouted; but the ice under Whitepaw's feet was so uncertain, he was afraid to hurry. Suddenly the ice under him began to sink. Whitepaw leaped for more solid footing. His forepaws made it, but his hindlegs went down into the river. Dwight dropped to the ice and reaching forward, grabbed Whitepaw by a foreleg, pulling him, dripping, back to safety.

Whitepaw stopped to shake the cold water from himself, but Dwight seized him by the scruff of the neck, and pulled him toward shore, scolding him as he did so. Whitepaw was so ashamed he couldn't look up, and he shook and shivered so violently, Dwight was sorry for him and quickly built a fire.

As Whitepaw sat near the fire, trembling with cold, Dwight held up a blanket behind him, to direct all the warmth upon him. Soon Whitepaw was fairly dry, and

Whitepaw shook and shivered violently.

to warm himself further, he began chasing wildly up and down the slope and around the shore.

Dwight called to him and giving him one of the sandwiches, he ate one himself, talking to Whitepaw, as he ate.

"Y'u got a' awful lot t' learn, Whitepaw," he kept

saying, throwing him a tiny piece of cooky as he did so.

After this meal they went on again, and for several hours they trudged along steadily and silently. Then, as the cold early winter evening began creeping into the air, a strange and unexpected feeling of fear took possession of Dwight. The river was so cold, the slopes so dismal in the deepening shadows of the trees, the atmosphere so uninhabited and lonely, the length of the night ahead of him seemed hardly endurable. He decided to go up the slope of the canyon, and on the flat lands above, try to locate some farm where he might be taken in for the night.

Coming up to the rim of the canyon, he picked his way through a rapidly darkening strip of woods, out upon a flat, stubbled field. There, in the indistinct distance, he made out the shrunken buildings of a little farm.

The light was fading so swiftly now, that by the time he came within a hundred yards of the place, the dusk was settling down into night. All along, as he had approached the farmyard, he had heard the barking of two dogs and it had worried him. He approached slowly, hoping that someone in the house would come out and hold them back. But there appeared to be no light in the house anywhere.

The barbed wire fence around the house was a considerable distance from it, and as Dwight did not care to try to crawl under or over the wires with his blankets and his bundles, he walked around toward the barbed wire gateway, which was on the opposite side. The gateway was extremely tight and as Dwight struggled with it, to open it, the two dogs came under the fence and fell upon Whitepaw, as if they were determined to kill him.

Dwight turned from the gate and attempted to drive the dogs off, but they paid little attention to him, until he had struck each one of them a whack with the butt of his rifle.

The snarling beasts shot back under the fence, but as Dwight moved on, deciding that the farmers were not at home, they followed along the fence, inside, showing signs of intending to leap out again at the first chance.

Dwight hurried along with Whitepaw at his heels, and when they were some distance off from the fenced-in farmyard, the vicious dogs behind them stopped barking and returned to their house.

Dwight walked rapidly back toward the river while there was still a trace of daylight in the air. This was a situation he had not foreseen. With Whitepaw at his side, he would find trouble like this at most farmyards, for all farmers had dogs.

When he got back to the river shore, he felt better. Somehow, the protecting walls of the canyon, the huge boulders, even the trees helped to give him a feeling of protection, like that of the walls of a room.

In the lea of one of these boulders which stood dark and massive against the sky-reflecting river beyond it, as if it had rolled down the canyon slope to its very base, Dwight gathered some driftwood and built a big fire; and, arranging a half-rotted windfall, he made himself a fairly comfortable seat beside it.

When the fire was going brightly, he made a thorough examination of Whitepaw, to see whether the dogs had torn his skin anywhere. But although Whitepaw had several matted spots on his fur, Dwight could find no wounds.

His loaded rifle in his right hand, his blankets over his shoulders, around himself and around Whitepaw who sat on his haunches between his knees, Dwight sat by his fire and peered into the thick shadows of the near distance, as his fire disturbed and moved them.

Mainly to hear a voice, he would break the oppressive stillness after long pauses, by talking to Whitepaw.

"If old Burnell 'd 'a' let me keep y'u with me, all the time, you'd 'a' growed up different, Whitepaw. You'd 'a' been a good watch dog. If you was a good watch dog, I c'd go t' sleep now, an' I'd know you'd wake me up, if somethin' come along. But Miss Martinby an' all the kids was all too good to y'u. You jus' like everything. You don't think anything's mean, Whitepaw. Y'u got t' watch out. Some things is very mean, an' want t' hurt you. Y'u got t' fight for y'urself. You should 'a' grabbed one o' those dogs b' the neck—y'u should 'a' ripped into 'em. If you'd 'a' grabbed one, I'd 'a' booted the other. You jus lay down, an' be friendly like. Y'u got t' fight for y'urself!"

As he went on talking, Dwight could feel Whitepaw's tail wagging against him. Now and then Whitepaw abruptly turned his muzzle up and licked at Dwight's face; but Dwight, still peering into the stirring shadows, was too serious, considering the long night ahead, to smile.

There were moments, as the night dragged on, when Dwight feared that he would not be able to endure it till morning, but even as he sat there, uncomfortably worrying about it, the moments slipped away as if a great clock somewhere beyond the silent black treetops were ticking them off, one by one.

CHAPTER VII

"... *Who Help Themselves*"

TOWARD morning, after he had piled his last pieces of driftwood within reach, on his fire, Dwight fell asleep out of sheer weariness. When he opened his eyes again, in the first faint light of daybreak, he had such a bad ache in his side and along his neck, that he jumped up and began rubbing himself. The fire was out and a cold dampness in the air discouraged any ideas of rebuilding it. He was sure he would feel better if they went on at once.

Before starting away, Dwight broke a hole in the ice a few feet off shore and took a big drink of water.

"Come on, Whitepaw," he said, "you better drink plenty. The sandwiches got t' last a long time."

By the time Dwight had rolled up his blankets and thrown them around his neck, the light had become enough stronger so that each rock and tree and windfall stood out separately, and they could pick their way along the cluttered shore without danger of tripping. And by the time full daylight had arched a silver-white sky over the great canyon, a sense of happy victory filled Dwight's heart.

He had overcome the greatest difficulty in his effort to get to Edmonton—the night. He was not afraid of hunger. He still had a little food, and he would find some game, today or tomorrow. He didn't mind the distance, because he had become a good walker on the Burnell farm. But he had been very much afraid of the long cold nights out in the open, and he had pulled through his first night, without anything harmful having befallen him. From now on, he would sleep unafraid, he was sure.

The sky was overcast, and the wind moaned and tugged, but Dwight plodded along steadily, unwilling to take time to chase the very few grouse and pheasants that appeared up on the canyon slopes. The shore was not so badly cluttered there, and he was making distance so well, he was determined to keep going. Even though Whitepaw began complaining, early in the afternoon, lifting a paw every now and then and shaking it, Dwight forged on resolutely.

But as soon as the late afternoon light began fading, Dwight stopped at a clutter of windfalls, and removing his blankets, set about preparing for the night. Gathering all the wood he could find, and laying out a good big fire, he proceeded to make himself a bed. Up at the rim of the canyon, there were some evergreen trees. Going up there, while Whitepaw, sore-footed, sat by the blankets and watched him, he gathered a huge armful of branches with needles on them and carried them down, spreading them out between a big log and his fire.

Before going to bed, Dwight divided what was left of his sandwiches, giving Whitepaw his share, a piece at a time. Whitepaw swallowed his food too greedily, without chewing it, and Dwight was deeply concerned about his health. He wanted no sick dog while they were on the way. When he cut a chunk of the cake and sat there eating it, he broke off pieces at intervals and threw them at Whitepaw, who had no trouble catching them by the light of the fire.

When darkness had settled down fully, Dwight stretched out on his bed of twigs and needles. But somehow, it wasn't quite as easy to go to sleep as he had thought it would be that morning, tired though he was. He lay there for a long time, listening so eagerly for sounds of anything which might approach, that in spite of his almost painful sleepiness, he was afraid to shut his eyes. However, he finally did fall asleep, and he slept so soundly, that it was quite light, when he awoke again. By the time the sun was up, he was sure that the following night he would sleep right through from the very first.

There were no more sandwiches for breakfast, and the fear that they would soon be hungry made Dwight reluctant about eating any of the cake he still had. Walking so continuously was hard labor and required plenty of food. Whitepaw constantly sniffed at the ground at every rock and tree-trunk, searching for something which might be eatable. Then, sometime toward noon, as Whitepaw approached a badly rotted windfall a part of it seemed to break away and with a frightening beating of wings, it sailed into the air and off to a stump halfway up the slope.

Whitepaw stopped dead still and looked after it, foolishly. He was about to start after it, when a growl-like order from Dwight froze him to the spot where he was standing, his tail stiff behind him, his head cocked, his ears pricked, his mouth open.

He saw Dwight creep forward a few feet, get down on hands and knees, and lift the gun he had been carrying with him. Suddenly he heard a terrible blast which broke the silence of the canyon and echoed back from the distance. Whitepaw was so frightened that he lowered himself to his stomach, but when he saw Dwight get up and race up the slope, he tore after him.

Dwight picked up the grouse by the legs and started down to the river shore with it. Whitepaw, half afraid of the dead bird, very suspicious now of the smoke-smelling gun, tried to sniff at it, as Dwight ran, swinging it.

At the river, Dwight quickly broke a hole in the ice, and prepared the huge grouse for broiling; then building a fire, he soon filled the air with tantalizing smells of broiling meat.

"Well, Whitepaw," cried Dwight, enthusiastically, as he threw him a hunk of broiled grouse, "if we c'n sleep out doors, an' shoot birds t' eat, we won't have t' beg any farmers f'r help."

Never had Whitepaw eaten anything so good in all his life. Hardly had Dwight given him one piece, before he was sitting up and looking beggingly at him again, asking for another.

"Gosh a'mighty, Whitepaw," said Dwight, "don't y'u chew even bones? Y'u mustn't be a hog, Whitepaw. You're a dog. Good gosh! I got t' chew *my* meat. If I'm goin' t' hand you a piece every time y'u sit there, ready f'r more, you'll be gettin' all of it."

Whitepaw licked his muzzle with embarrassment, wriggled uncomfortably, wagged his tail feebly and looked so sorry for himself that Dwight threw him another piece.

The grouse had been a big bird for its kind, but it didn't last very long between the two of them. And when they put out the fire and walked on again, Whitepaw ran on ahead, sniffing at every stump with brightest hopes that there he might scare up another grouse.

But while there were evidences of grouse and pheasants, Dwight took no time to hunt. Falling into a steady pace, he trudged along mile after mile, until darkness again lowered into the river canyon.

Once more Dwight prepared himself a bed of twigs. This night he fell asleep as soon as he stretched out; and at the first peep of dawn, they were on their way again.

As he walked along at a steady pace, Dwight figured that they had averaged at least twenty-five miles a day. This meant that they should now be more than half way to Edmonton. The aches and pains of the first few days seemed to have vanished, and the blisters on his feet had stopped tormenting him, even though they hurt, every time he stepped on a stone or twisted a foot. He felt quite tired of walking, but he minded it less now, and he felt that he was going much faster. Making more distance, he disliked more than ever stopping to look for game, hoping that Whitepaw, who always trotted on slightly ahead, might scare up another bird.

But in the middle of the afternoon, becoming very hungry again, Dwight climbed up to the rim of the canyon, to see what he might find on the stubbled lands above, where prairie chicken often raked the stubble for the grain which had been dropped at harvesting.

The woodland strip which followed the rim of the river canyon was not very thick at that point, and Dwight could see a stubbled field through the few scattered trees. Coming out to that field, he saw a quarter of a mile away a solitary straw stack; and it seemed to Dwight that he saw a bird lift from the ground near the stack, then alight again. Motioning Whitepaw to stay behind him, Dwight got his gun ready, dropped his blankets and moved on toward the straw stack cautiously.

Whitepaw followed close behind, tense with excitement. Suddenly Dwight ordered Whitepaw to stop and lowering himself to the ground, he crept forward a hundred feet or so and stopped. Whitepaw saw him lift the gun and at once he heard the awful blast he had heard the day before. When Dwight got up and leaped like a rabbit toward the strawstack, Whitepaw leaped after him.

Dwight picked up a big, beautifully colored pheasant rooster; and gathering his blankets, started back to the river, where, before a roaring fire, they were soon feasting on broiled pheasant.

By the time they had finished with their meal, it was getting dark.

"Know it, Whitepaw," said Dwight thoughtfully, "a straw stack's a mighty soft bed. I'm too tired t' go lookin' f'r boughs. Let's hike back up there to that straw pile, an' have a good night's sleep; an' in the morning, maybe, we might get another rooster f'r breakfast."

The day had been a cloudy one, and the night came down fast and heavy. By the time they got to the straw stack, Dwight was glad that he didn't have to spend this night along the river.

When he had climbed to the top of the stack Dwight looked around cautiously, but no farmyard lights were

Whitepaw followed close behind.

visible anywhere. So he proceeded to beat out a long-ish, oblong hole in the straw, digging somewhat to the side, once he got below the surface, so as to have some of the straw reach over them. Then covering himself with his blankets, he told Whitepaw to lie down, partly over his feet, and went to sleep.

It was the softest bed he had had since he had left the teacher's house, but it was colder this night, and the broiled meat, good as it had been, hadn't agreed any too well with him. At least he thought that that was what was ailing him, for Dwight felt a bit dizzy and feverish, and when he breathed deeply, he felt slight pains in his lungs.

During the night the wind blew up so hard, its moaning around the straw stack woke him up. It sounded like some poor thing lost out somewhere in the darkness, and it bothered him.

When he awoke at dawn, his head was aching, and a strange weakness had come over him. Slightly frightened, he roused himself, deciding that walking on might make him feel better.

The straw stack was covered white with frost, as was every stalk in the stubbled field around it; and it looked in the half light of early morning, as if the winter had descended upon them during the night. When they got down to the river and went out upon the ice to get a drink, Dwight saw that the river was now frozen clear across.

This feeling of winter and snow which was in the air made Dwight anxious to be on his way. He filled up with water, but he was unable to induce Whitepaw to drink any. When he started away, he lunged forward into a steady, determined pace which he did not break for a moment until early in the afternoon. He was beating along in this dogged steadiness when he was startled by a bit of sunlight, and looking up into the gloomy gray sky, he saw that the sun had broken through. But a short space to either side of the sun itself, glowed alarming, tell-tale sundogs. Farmers had told him that sun dogs were a sure sign of a blizzard coming.

For more than an hour, Dwight tramped along, trying to make up his mind whether to go up to the flatlands above the canyon, or to take his chances continuing along the river shore. But when snowflakes began falling at early dusk, he turned abruptly and hurried up the incline, Whitepaw trotting wearily behind him.

He was worried, on reaching the rim of the canyon, to find the woods there unusually thick. For some time he continued southward, peering eagerly through the gloom for signs of open country; then, deciding that the forest might go on like that for many miles, and preferring to spend the night in the lea of some boulder near the river shore to that dismal forest with the winds howling through the trees, he turned again and picked his way back, against the cruelly penetrating north wind which had been increasing in violence all afternoon.

By the time he got back to the river, the flakes were whirling so thickly he decided to find the best possible shelter at once and gather enough wood for a fire, before the snow made it too wet to burn.

He came to an overhanging rock jutting out from the side of the canyon wall, which was so steep there that it was almost vertical. The rock was covered with bushes and along one side there were several large trees fallen upon each other, and the ground under them was covered with a pile of their dead branches.

Under the rock and near the clutter of twigs and branches, Dwight cleared a space and proceeded to build a fire. But the snow was now falling thick and fast, and even under the protection of the boulder, the flakes wet the shavings he made as fast as he could whittle them. He was painfully weary and not at all well, and the struggle to get his fire going exasperated him. No sooner did he have a little flame going than the vicious wind would whirl around and put it out; and beyond the reaches of the boulder the river shore was fast covering up with dead winter whiteness. To get his fire started, it was necessary for him to hold a blanket up against the blast.

When he finally got his fire going fairly brightly, Dwight wrapped the blankets about him, over his head, and sat down on a log against the rock, Whitepaw between his knees, in front of him.

He was sure that his fire would not last very long, however, for every once in a while the blasts with a sudden surge of fury would change direction and lash in under the rock with a wail and a whistle and go tearing away up the river, leaving his tiny flames trembling for very existence.

And the fury of the storm was not all that worried Dwight as he sat there shivering with fear as well as cold. He was not well, he knew, and he kept trying his throat by swallowing, and trying his lungs by breathing deeply to see whether they still hurt. He was afraid to go to sleep.

Soon the last of the flames began to sizzle, but Dwight made no effort to replenish his fire. The effort now seemed too much for him.

The temperature was not as low as it had been the night before, but it was too cold for one sitting on a log, without a fire. Yet while Dwight felt disagreeably cold, as the fire died down, he was also strangely hot, and from time to time he reached out and took handfuls of snow and ate it, to cool his throat.

The night seemed endless. It was the worst night he had ever had to endure. He would slip off into sleep and rouse himself soon after with the fear that in his sleep he would freeze to death. Whitepaw, between his knees and close to him, kept him alive, the warmth issuing from him as from a little stove.

When dawn came at last, Dwight found it almost impossible to stir; and it was more than an hour after the first signs of daybreak, before he prevailed upon himself to attempt to stand up. When he started to roll up his blankets, the effort almost dizzied him; but he realized that now he must reach some farm house or die, and slowly lifting a foot at a time, he began plowing away along the snow-covered shore, occasionally turning wearily to make sure Whitepaw was behind him.

The struggle in that deep snow, at first, appeared impossible, but as Dwight exerted himself, and daylight increased, some of his strength came back to him. Pulling out one foot and sinking down with the other, he moved along for several hours. Then he came to where the canyon slopes flattened away, completely. An avenue about a hundred yards wide broke through the forest southward, leading to a ridge half a mile away, the whiteness of which almost blended into the murky sky.

Dwight stopped, and breathing rapidly, studied the whiteness a moment. It looked as if there might be a roadway along the opening through the forest. While

the ridge seemed so far away that the thought of plowing up the incline brought tears to his eyes, the hope
that it would lead him to some farmhouse, sent him
bravely groping through the deep snows.

And he was really groping now. As he laboriously
pulled a foot out of the snow, only to sink into it a few
inches farther, the weariness that was upon him and
the lashing of the wind, made him shut his eyes, and
he crept along as in a nightmare. Then, one time as he
opened his eyes after a few moments' rest, before attempting to extricate himself again, he saw Whitepaw
sitting a few rods ahead of him on the surface of the
snow, looking to the right into a clump of trees, as if
he were seeing something that interested him.

"Maybe there's a house in there," thought Dwight;
and with the hope and excitement came the energy
with which to pull his way out.

As soon as Dwight came to within a few feet from
Whitepaw, Whitepaw started forward to the side, and
toward the clump of trees. Painfully creeping after him,
Dwight came to an open space which hardened under
his feet. It was a roadway, he realized, from which the
wind had swept much of the snow. Walking so much
more easily along the road, Dwight soon reached the
clump of trees, and there, some two hundred yards
ahead of him, he saw a house.

Where the trees shut away some of the wind, the
snow was deep again, but now he was only a few yards
from the house. In front of him was a pile of wood, all
but the top pieces covered with snow. To the right of
the pile of wood was the house, and to the left of it a

small barn. Whitepaw was eagerly sniffing around the snow-covered platform before the door, looking back at Dwight repeatedly, as if urging him to hurry.

But Dwight's first flush of hope gave way to a sense of fear. There was an unmistakable air of desertion about the place, clear even in the distance. The moment he took hold of the door knob, he knew that that door hadn't been opened in weeks. Everywhere the white, fluffy snow lay thick and soft and untouched.

Dwight trudged all the way around the house, but there was no other door, and the windows appeared frozen fast, if they weren't locked.

Back at the door, Dwight stopped. He was desperate. Going on to look for another house seemed impossible, sick and weak as he was.

A few inches to the side of the door was a window and as Dwight looked at it, it occurred to him that if the house was an unused one, he would find very little comfort there, even if he did get in. Scraping the snow away from one of the panes, he breathed upon it and peered in. He couldn't see very clearly, but he thought he saw a stove. A stove and a fire inside would save his life.

Dwight looked down at Whitepaw. Whitepaw was watching him and dancing around nervously as if he couldn't understand why Dwight foolishly hesitated about opening the door and going in.

"A person has a right t' save his life, Whitepaw," he said.

Turning back to the window, it occurred to him that if he broke out one of the panes, he could put his arm through and open the lock on the door, from the inside.

He turned around and looked away up the road with the instinctive fear of someone possibly coming. The idea of breaking into a house was revolting to him, but for all he knew there might not be another house for miles. How could he possibly go on struggling through those awful snows? His own words came ringing back into his mind: "A person has a right t' save himself."

With the stock of his gun, he struck the window pane a sharp blow, and the broken glass crashed on the floor inside. Then, heart thumping wildly, he reached in and opened the door.

Whitepaw leaped in as if that were where he had lived all his life. Dwight walked in hesitatingly. He found himself in a narrow kitchen across the entire width of the house, and through a wide open door he saw that there was only one other room to the house, a large living room with a fireplace at the other end.

The air in the kitchen was musty, as in a place that had been closed up a long time; but everything was clean and orderly. The wood box, beside the large range, was filled to the top with dry wood and kindling. And when he took the lid off to see about starting a fire, he discovered that there was paper and kindling and wood in it, ready to be lighted.

After he had lighted the fire, Dwight walked to the open doorway to the next room and looked in. He saw Whitepaw near the fireplace sniffing around at things and eyeing the big bull moose head high above the fireplace. The walls of the room were literally covered with hunting pictures and trophies, including several beautifully stuffed China pheasant roosters.

The wide space before the fireplace was cluttered with well pillowed chairs and rockers and between these and the doorway where he was standing, Dwight saw two large beds, one on each side, neatly spread with heavy quilts and blankets.

Dwight turned back into the kitchen. On the stove which was already radiating heat through the musty coldness, there was a copper teakettle, and near the sink, to the side of the tall cupboard, he saw a pump. The teakettle was empty, and the pump wouldn't draw water; so he went out and filled the kettle with snow. When the snow was melted on the stove, he primed the pump with the warm water.

He was greatly relieved by the feeling that he had saved himself, that he would have a comfortable place to sleep, but he was still not feeling at all well as he moved about the kitchen. Whenever he had had a cold at the Burnell's, Mrs. Burnell used to give him a mixture of hot water and milk with plenty of sugar in it; so he decided that if he found nothing better, he might at least drink plenty of hot water.

When he opened the cupboard to look for a cup, he found a whole set of dishes and silverware. Encouraged by this find, he began searching further. Opening a door in one of the small cupboards along the floor, below the dish closet, he found row upon row of all sorts of canned goods. There were tin boxes of crackers in the next cupboard and two huge tins, containing flour. In one place he found a large ham and several slabs of bacon; and in the last little cupboard he saw a small wooden barrel filled with what looked like dog biscuits.

Everything was packed against rats and arranged with an orderliness which worried Dwight. He resolved to take only what Whitepaw and he absolutely needed, and when he was able to go on, to leave the place as orderly as he had found it. Yet when he took a handful of dog biscuits and threw them to the floor for White-paw, he experienced a deep sense of guilt.

"Soon's I find some paper," he muttered, as White-paw gobbled the biscuits, "we'll make a list of everything we take. When I find work in Edmonton, I'll pay it all back."

The wind outdoors was increasing steadily, and the draft reminded him of the broken window. He must fix that somehow, because the snow was piling in on the floor. In the tall kitchen cabinet he had noticed a board that he could pull out, on which there were signs of flour, where dough had been kneaded. Taking this out, he quickly fastened it against the open window, shuddering as he looked out into the swirling atmosphere with the thought of what might have happened to them if they hadn't stumbled upon this hunting lodge.

The fireplace, like the stove, was laid for a fire. Starting a quick blaze, Dwight returned to the kitchen where he opened one of the cans and warmed himself some soup in a pan. When he got back to the fireplace with his bowl of soup and some crackers, the fire was roaring up the black throat of the chimney. He sat down in one of the comfortable chairs, in front of the fire, and eating his soup slowly, threw a cracker to Whitepaw now and then.

In spite of the dismal raging of the storm outdoors, the room became warm enough for Dwight to remove his sheepskin coat and his cap. The soup warming him inside, the fire glowing upon him cozily, not having slept properly for several days, Dwight sank into a deep sleep.

When he woke again it was night. The frost on the windows was white only where it reflected the dim light from the fireplace; and, except for the still-glowing fire, the room was pitch dark. Outdoors an angry wind was shaking the house and moaning against the corners.

Dwight felt too weak to bother looking for a lamp, and, replenishing the fire and getting his two blankets, he wrapped them around his shoulders and went back to sleep on the chair. He didn't like the idea of using one of the beds. Whitepaw curled himself up at his feet, and with a sigh of luxurious contentment, returned to his own interrupted slumbers.

There Dwight remained, sleeping and waking in snatches, worrying about having broken into a house that didn't belong to him, yet thanking his lucky stars that he was not out in the open.

CHAPTER VIII

Snow-bound

ALL night long the winds lashed and tore at the hunting lodge, moaning and shrieking at the eaves and wailing away through the snow-packed forest, showers of hard, cold snow rasping down the slants of the roof, the blasts occasionally seizing the entire lodge and shaking it, as if they meant to shake the life out of it, its seasoned boards creaking dismally in protest. By morning, the full fury of a north-Canadian blizzard had settled itself upon the country to stay. The windows were completely covered with frost and further half-covered with snow, and the light that trickled in through them was like twilight.

But Dwight managed to keep the fireplace glowing with good cheer. The wood boxes built to serve as seats on both sides of the fireplace were filled with three-foot logs; and he promised himself that as soon as he felt better and the storm died out, he would refill these boxes, if at all possible.

But as this new day wore along past noon, he found that he was not feeling any better. In fact, much as he tried to assure himself that he would soon be strong again, he was steadily growing weaker. He did very little cooking because he did not have the energy to

move around, and most of the little he cooked, he gave
to Whitepaw.

All afternoon he sat there drowsing, looking into the
fire and trying to assure himself that he would be ready
to go on the next day. Toward evening, he decided to
cook some of the ham, feeling that if he ate something
substantial, he would regain his strength. But moving
around made him dizzy, and so, feeding Whitepaw, he
undressed and got into one of the two beds.

He slept quite soundly, and when he awoke in the
morning daylight was already oozing through the frost-
covered windows. Dwight started to get up, but he was
alarmed by the strange sense of weakness that had come
over him; and when he breathed, his chest hurt him.
The fire had gone out and the room was cold. Afraid,
however, that if he stayed in bed, he might soon be
unable to get up at all, he got up and dressed.

He built himself a fire in the fireplace, and sitting
down in its comforting warmth, sat there all day long,
exerting himself only to replenish the fire or to feed
Whitepaw. At dusk he got into bed again. He didn't
sleep very well, but when he got up in the morning, he
thought he felt very much better.

He made himself a good breakfast, and enjoyed sitting by the fire all morning. At noon he was hungry
enough to eat a hearty meal, and the feeling that he
was getting well made him very happy. That afternoon
was the happiest he had ever known, sitting by the fire
and dreaming of doing the vague, fine things Miss Martinby had assured him he was capable of doing. He
would find work which would enable him to also go

to school, and he would study in the way which he had learned to study and enjoy books, under her kindly direction.

He went to bed anxious to be on his way again. He would get up very early and after breakfast, would take one of the big saws hanging in the corner of the kitchen and would go out and find enough wood to refill the woodboxes. Then he would have a substantial, early lunch, and cleaning up the lodge, start off as near noon as possible, going by way of the road, so that in case he needed help he might find a farm house where he could ask for it.

When he got up in the morning, however, and after his breakfast began to refill the woodbox near the kitchen stove, he realized that he was not really strong enough yet for traveling through heavy snows; and he decided to put in another day in rest. Again he enjoyed sitting by the fire all afternoon and again he went to bed with the feeling that next morning he must start on his way.

When, however, right after his early breakfast, he started out with the saw, he looked blankly into a snowy world, blazing with the early sun. The snows everywhere were several feet deep, and the evergreen-tree branches were hanging low with their heavy loads of sparkling whiteness. It was impossible for him to get any wood, under so much snow.

On the ledge of the cupboard lay the sheet of paper on which he had kept his list of the food he had eaten up. Taking it, Dwight added: About twenty logs—three feet long. When he got to Edmonton, he would ask

Miss Martinby to help him find out who the owner of this lodge was. As soon as he got himself a job, he would start paying for all he had used, including the window-pane which he had broken.

His decision made, Dwight went happily about straightening up the place as best he could, and sweeping the floors. The exertion dizzied him considerably again; but he was determined not to give in to this weakness.

Again he rolled up the extra clothes he had brought with him in his blankets ready to start away. He was just throwing them around his neck, when Whitepaw who had been watching him, suddenly leaped forward and began to bark. Dwight froze with fear and his lower jaw dropped; and as he listened with beating heart, he heard sleigh-bells jingling.

By the time he had gotten his gun and opened the door, the cutter which seemed to have come up from the river, had turned toward the lodge. The horses were beautiful and lively; and two men were seated in the cutter, which drove right up to the woodpile and stopped.

When he saw a tall man, in a long fur coat, jump angrily from the cutter seat and start toward him, Dwight was paralyzed. The man approached carefully, however, his eyes going from the gun to the dog.

"What are you doing here?" he demanded, stopping at a respectful distance.

Dwight began to speak, intending to explain how he had come up the river, how he had gotten caught in the blizzard, and how he had become sick. But true as all this was, he was suddenly overcome by the feeling that it would be impossible to convince the man of it.

"You better drop that gun," said the man.

Dwight obediently handed the gun to him. The fellow seemed less angry when he took it, and he walked into the house. Dwight could hear him walk all around the place, inside. In the meantime, the second man got off the cutter and started unhooking the horses, silently.

Coming out again to the doorway, the first man shouted to the second: "The little thief's eaten up most of our supplies and used up all our dry wood!"

"I didn't steal it," pleaded Dwight. "I'm goin' t' Edmonton an' I'm going t' get work an' pay for it all."

"What were you doing here?"

"I couldn't go on in the blizzard—I was sick."

"Sick!" cried the angry man, mockingly. "Two miles up the road, here, is a farm—why didn't you go there?"

"I didn't know there was," muttered Dwight, feeling dizzy again.

The second man, who had by this time unhooked the two horses, holding them by their bridle-bits, came toward Dwight to get a better look at him.

"This is the third time in two years that this place has been broken into," said the first man to the second, who did not answer; then he turned to Dwight. "I'm going to make an example of you."

"I'm going to work in Edmonton," muttered Dwight, unconvincingly, "an' I'll pay it all back."

"You can settle that with the judge," said the man. "You come along with me."

Angrily, he seized Dwight by the arm, taking a cautious look meantime at Whitepaw. But Whitepaw merely looked slightly puzzled and started patiently to follow them.

The man led them to the barn, the second man following close behind with the two horses, and unlocking the door, he shoved Dwight in.

"You can stay in this barn," he said, "until I'm ready to take you into town. You can sleep on the hay."

The barn was cold and dark. Beyond the three roomy stalls, in front, was a wooden platform on which there was a pile of hay which reached to the very ceiling at the farthest end. As Dwight made his way forlornly to the hay, the man called after him: "Don't you try to run away, because——"

He stopped. The second man had come to the door with the two horses, and they began to whisper to each other.

"You better take your boots off," said the first man again, coming up to Dwight who was now on the pile of hay, on the platform.

"I was awful sick," began Dwight again, as he proceeded to take a boot off, but he could see that the man was angered by his attempt to explain; and so he removed the other boot in silence.

The man picked up the boots and went off to the house with them. The second man tied the horses in their stalls and gave them some hay, removing their harness from their backs. Then he tied a heavy blanket around each of the fine-looking horses, and went out, carefully shutting the barn door behind him.

Dwight wrapped his own blankets around him and

with Whitepaw beside him, sat there trying to think
of what he ought to do. Why had it been so hard to
convince this man, he wondered. He was telling the
truth. He had always thought that telling the truth
would convince anybody. When they were taking him
in to the judge in Edmonton, he would beg them to
first let him see Miss Martinby. She would understand
and she would convince this fellow that he was telling
the truth. "A person's got the right t' save himself."

When he grew weary sitting there on the hay,
Dwight fixed himself a bed and lay down, hoping that
he would fall asleep and sleep the awful hours away.

Whitepaw could not understand the whole business
at all. The fact that Dwight remained in the barn and
on the hay, was enough to make him feel that that was
where he himself belonged. But he kept thinking of the
house and the comfortable fire, and he kept hoping that
Dwight would get up and walk back with him into the
lodge.

In time he became painfully bored, just sitting there,
while Dwight slept, and he moved off into the rest of
the barn to get acquainted with the two horses. The
horses were no friendlier than the men. As soon as he
approached a stall and sniffed, as inoffensively as possible, they began to stamp around angrily, and look back
with fear in their large round eyes.

The barn door was locked, so he couldn't go outdoors, and after going completely around the barn,
sniffing at everything, he returned to Dwight on the
hay. There he curled up and lay until he could not

endure lying there any longer; then he got up and went sniffing all around the barn again.

The twilight in the barn grew into deep darkness. The first man came along with some good-smelling meat sandwiches for Dwight, but Dwight contemptuously refused them, whereupon the man merely laid them down on the hay beside him. When he was gone, Dwight gave the sandwiches to Whitepaw. But when the man came back again with a warm drink for Dwight and a bone and a tin of water for him, Whitepaw thought he was a very kind man.

It didn't take Whitepaw long to tear off what meat there was on the bone; but having nothing else to do, since Dwight was sleeping all the time and coughing repeatedly at intervals, Whitepaw spent most of the long, tedious night, working upon it.

Soon after the coming of daylight, the first man came into the barn again, bringing a plate on which there was some good-smelling bacon and an egg. When Dwight refused to get up and eat it, the man's voice seemed to become kinder than it had been at any time. But while Whitepaw hoped that something good would come out of the change it implied, Dwight only coughed and continued to lie there, as the man looked down at him.

After the man walked out, Dwight moved the plate with the bacon and the egg over to Whitepaw, and the second man, coming in to feed the horses, saw him do it.

"What are you doing that for, you silly boy?" he cried. "Why don't you eat it yourself?"

Just then, the first man came back carrying Dwight's boots.

"Put your boots on," he said, "and come into the lodge."

Dwight coughed, but he didn't move.

"Come on, son," said the man persuasively, "I'm *not* going to report you to the police. I found the paper on which you had the list of the things you took, and I'm convinced now that you really meant to pay for it all."

Dwight sat up, his fever-racked eyes dilating.

"The paper," he said, feeling at the pocket of his coat.

"You left it on the cupboard," said the man. "Come, put your boots on."

Dwight reached over wearily and took one of the boots, but sat there holding it a moment.

"Let me help you," said the man, getting down on his knees in the hay.

But when the man had put his boots on for him, and Dwight attempted to stand, his legs couldn't hold him up. The man caught him.

"Len," he called to the second man, "better hitch up the horses; I'll have to take him into town to the hospital."

The horses were quickly hitched to the cutter; and wrapped around with his blankets, Dwight was seated next to the driver, a heavy fur robe thrown over his lap.

As the cutter turned and started away toward the river, Whitepaw raced after it, galloping along on the side where Dwight was sitting. At the river, he was surprised to see the cutter go right out upon the ice, as if they were going to cross to the other side. Out near the middle of the river, however, the horses turned westward and continued trotting parallel with the shorelines, where the winds had blown most of the snow away.

Whitepaw hadn't forgotten his first experience with that ice, and he went out upon it with great hesitation; but the cutter didn't wait for him. It moved so far off away from him that in fear of losing it, he braved the ice. A few moments of tremblingly feeling his way toward the center of the river, and he became more confident. When he finally caught up to the cutter, he kept so close to its rounded back, that, had it stopped, he would have bumped into it. His frightened eyes on the swift runners before him, the breath pouring out of his mouth like smoke, he followed the thing mile after mile.

The snow was too cold and dry to cake a great deal, but he was obliged every once in a while to lie down and bite away what had gathered under one or two of his paws. And always after this operation, he had to gallop with all his might, to catch up to the sleigh again.

As the sun, toward noon, came out and softened the surface of the snows, he was obliged to drop out more and more often to bite the caked snow away from his paws, and each time the cutter gained some distance on him. To add to the struggle, the sun's glare on the snow reflected back and burned into his eyes. His tongue lolling out of his mouth, his legs aching, his head swimming, he dropped farther and farther behind.

Then early in the afternoon, the sun covered by passing clouds, he got his second wind; and little by little the distance between him and the cutter shortened again.

From time to time, they began passing houses, up along the rim of the canyon, or even where the shore was level up to the canyon slope. The more houses they passed, the more dogs Whitepaw began hearing. He hadn't forgotten the vicious dogs at the farmyard up on the flats above the canyon, the first night out from the teacher's house. If he happened to slip back any distance from the sleigh, the faraway barking of a dog would drive him forward with renewed energy.

Late in the afternoon, when the short winter day began darkening, the houses began to increase in number along the lip of the canyon. In places, groups of them began to appear on ledges, along the middle or the lower half of the slopes; and the air seemed to fill up with the disagreeable, staccato hammerings of distant dogs.

At times he heard the shouts of children at play which reminded Whitepaw of the happy recess times in the school yard. Sometimes when the noises of city life frightened him he would pull out to the side, to look up and make sure that Dwight was still in the seat beside the driver. But while Dwight was still in his seat, he seemed strangely indifferent to him, never looking down or calling to him.

The cold, waning daylight turned into colder twilight. The city noises and smells became so strong they were stifling to Whitepaw. One time, now more badly in need of assurances that Dwight was still there, as Whitepaw leaped out to the side to look, he saw a black smear across the wintry spaces before him. It was the span of a great iron bridge stretching from one canyon lip to the other. The flats above the canyon in both directions were cluttered with houses and buildings, streams of smoke rising from many chimneys.

Frightened by this bridge which was roaring with the automobiles that were racing across it, he hurried back, behind the cutter, keeping so close as they passed under the bridge, that his muzzle touched the back of it.

A few feet beyond the noisy bridge, the sleigh turned to the right and slid across the ice to the shore, slithering over the snow drifts on the shore, and starting up the incline more slowly. At the top of the slope, it broke through a cleft in the rim of the canyon, and came to a dead stop at the street which ran parallel with the canyon.

As Whitepaw peered into the street, along the side of the cutter, his eyes were fairly popping out of his head. Beyond the stream of traffic, he saw what appeared to him a great formless cluster of window lights, like golden stars; while on the street itself, whole multitudes of automobiles were racing in both directions, their lights like protruding eyes, glaring at him with spear-like beams, their wheels grinding the snow, their chains clanking angrily, their horns blaring arrogantly, dust rising in showers from the constantly churned snow.

Suddenly the cutter lunged forward again. Amazed by what he was seeing, Whitepaw was caught off guard. He made a nervous attempt to race after it, but before he could get to it, one of the automobiles broke in, in front of him. He shrank back out of its way; but when it had passed, the cutter was gone. In the yawning chasm before him, two opposing streams of automobiles now poured along, obstructing his way. One monstrous car bore down upon him from one side, its ogre eyes glaring right at him, the front wheel looming up over him, its horn rasping angrily. Whitepaw was too frightened even to attempt to get out of its way. As he crouched down, the wheels veered, and the machine went whizzing by him, the fender striking him sharply on the nose.

The sting of that blow lasted several minutes. By the time he dared to try again to cross the street, another car bore down upon him, the one behind it almost running over him, as he stepped back to get out of its way. In abject terror, he crept back into the cleft in the rim of the canyon.

Head high with fear and anxiety, eyes blazing, nose vibrating, his forelegs trembling, his tail between his legs, Whitepaw came sneaking back to peer again into whirlpool of machines and lights.

Along the edge of the canyon was a sidewalk, its flat cold slabs dug out of the snow which was piled in long ridges on each side, running like a white ditch as far as the eye could see in both directions. As Whitepaw sat there sniffing the air and peering into the welter of lights and moving vehicles, he suddenly became aware of something, coming down the sidewalk between the two ridges of snow. He turned and faced a golden collie with a longish, cruel muzzle, tail stiff behind him, less than a dozen feet away and coming unmistakably at him.

He turned and faced a fierce-looking collie.

Whitepaw leaped for the cleft in the canyon rim and down the trail on which he had come up from the river, the collie right after him, nipping his rump as he ran.

Bewildered as Whitepaw was by this unwarranted attack, he had the sense to try to get under or into something. Instead of going all the way down to the river, he swerved about fifty feet from the top, to the side, and ducked into the shadows under the bridge. As he swept around one part of the concrete base of the steel supports of the bridge, he saw a narrow niche in the concrete. Quickly he pushed himself into it, backward, in order to face the collie. But as he lay there panting, listening and glaring into the descending darkness, the collie did not appear.

Exhausted by this time, Whitepaw curled up, his face and his ears outward, so that he could guard against the possible return of the collie, his heart pounding so loudly in the blood vessels near his ears that he could hardly separate the noises that came from the street from those that ground on the bridge overhead. A feeling of hatred for the collie who prevented his looking for Dwight, lighted up in his muddled brain like a fire.

So long as the fear of the collie lasted, he remained in his niche; but as the moments went by without the collie's return, his anxiety about finding Dwight welled up again, and venturing out of his hiding, Whitepaw cautiously crept up the trail to the cleft in the rim of the canyon wall.

There he sat for hours, watching against the possible return of the collie, peering into the traffic, afraid to attempt to cross that street now, even when the traffic had largely died out. When the temperature sank so low that he could not endure to sit there any longer, he picked his way back to the niche in the concrete base of the bridge support, where, in abject misery, he spent his first night in Edmonton, alone.

CHAPTER IX

Dogs, Too, Must Eat

IN THE small dark hours of the early winter morning, Whitepaw was startled by the jingling of sleigh bells. He jumped to his feet and tore down the incline, going so fast that he tripped over a bushtop which stuck up out of the snow crust, and went over on his back, sliding halfway down the incline before he was able to right himself.

With a shower of snow dust rising from the horses' hoofs, the sleigh swept by his nose, on its way down to the river, where on the roadway, along the center of the ice, it turned westward. It was not only *not* going in the direction he had come from, but it was a longish bob sleigh, not very much like the cutter Dwight had been on. He was painfully disappointed, but he couldn't bear to give up, and so he followed it, vaguely hoping some miracle might suddenly turn it into the cutter he wanted so much to see.

On account of an abnormal amount of snow, many of the Edmonton groceries and dairies made their deliveries in the suburbs and along the canyon, with bob sleighs.

A quarter of a mile west of the bridge, the sleigh turned shoreward again and up the slope. Whitepaw, running hungrily along a few feet behind, slowed down, his eyes taking in a row of houses on a ledge along the canyon wall.

The sleigh came to a stop at the first of the houses. Whitepaw sat down on his haunches and watched the driver jump from his seat. He listened to the crunching of the man's boots as he went up the steps to the porch, and he saw him, dark as it was, set something white down on the porch floor. When the man went on to the next house, Whitepaw crept toward the porch and sniffed at it.

It was milk and Whitepaw was very hungry. He reached toward the bottle, carefully, and licked it. It tasted good, what little he had found to taste; but just then he heard a dog bark, a few houses away. Still hurting where the collie had nipped him, he slunk down to the river again and back to his niche in the concrete base of the bridge support.

Little by little, the light grew stronger. The city life and traffic became more and more active and noisy; and again Whitepaw cautiously made his way out to the open slope. On the snow trail, going up to the rim of the canyon, he picked up a very faint scent of the horses of the hunting lodge. At once he went racing up to the street above and the swirling traffic in which Dwight had disappeared. There he began his long and faithful watch.

Look as he would, however, the cutter did not come back. When the sun rose over a mass of treetops, Whitepaw picked out a sunny spot on the sidewalk, and lay down in such a way that he would be sure to see the collie, were he to come again to attack him.

At first, as soon as anybody came walking along the sidewalk, Whitepaw would get up and slink down the canyon slope. But after a while, finding that people didn't even look at him, he began to stay where he was, watching them alertly as they passed. Then, after a few had thrown a kindly greeting at him in passing, he began

There he began his long and faithful watch.

to sniff at them and wag his tail. But always, after each passer-by, he would reach up on the snow ridge with his forepaws and gaze anxiously into the traffic of the street.

All day long Whitepaw watched there, moving off a few feet only when he became too restless lying or sitting still, or when hunger urged him to go search for food. When the increased traffic at the close of the day had given way to the peaceful hum of night, and the cold darkness filled the canyon to the very top, Whitepaw in despair withdrew to his niche in the concrete base of the bridge support. There he curled up as tight as he could and lay shivering miserably through the second night.

So cold was he all night long, that when the sun finally came out again, he spent most of the following day on sunny spots on the sidewalk, trying to thaw himself out. So long as there was a sunny spot anywhere, Whitepaw dozed in it; and one time the collie was almost upon him, before he was aware of him. Again the unfriendly beast chased him all the way back to his niche.

The temperature, which had been dropping steadily, went down so low when night came again that Whitepaw could not endure the idea of shivering in his cold, concrete niche. He was so hungry, too, that he couldn't have been contented to lie there, even if it had been less cold than it was.

The canyon slopes were lighted up by the many lights of the bridge, reflected back from the snows. The bushtops sticking up from the crust offered some protection, in case he was obliged to dash for cover, so Whitepaw went searching for food, lured by the memory of the milk bottle on the porch.

He followed the irregular shoreline westward, moving but a few feet at a time, repeatedly sitting down on his haunches to survey the slopes, especially the upper edge of the canyon where, he felt, the collie lived.

When he came to a point, directly below the first row of houses on the ledge, he saw a lamp gleaming through one of the side windows, which made him think of the teacher's house. Slowly, he crept toward it, sitting down every few feet and sniffing in every direction.

The night was very cold and very still. Only creatures without homes, like himself, were out. The snow crust was hard and smooth and sparkling. When the slightest little breeze arose for a moment, it would break off a frost-encrusted twig, here and there, and send it rolling down the white surfaces. Whitepaw would turn his head and watch these move, till they stopped. Every once in a while, a trolley car would go grinding across the distant bridge.

When these noises stopped, he would move another few feet nearer to the house and again sit down and sniff. The lamplight in the window had led him there in the first place, but now something else was drawing him powerfully. There were now unmistakable food smells in the cruelly biting, cold air. He crept closer and closer, moving around in a semicircle, now approaching the blind, windowless side of the house.

As he came within the shadow of the blind wall, he realized that the food smells were coming from the other side of the shed, which was back of the house. He didn't like to get caught between the house and the shed, so he stole around the upper side of the house and came down the slope, past the house; and a few feet from the corner of the shed he saw a dog lying near a large can which had been turned over on its side. The dog was obviously gnawing on a bone.

If Whitepaw hadn't been so completely surprised as to lose, for the moment, all power of moving, he would have fled. But not only did the dog seem peacefully busy, but the smell of food was now so strong, from that close range, it held him as with a rope.

Whitepaw licked his chops. His eyes peering at the

overturned pail, he began to whine. The dog heard him and quickly got to its feet. It wasn't at all the great big, golden collie. It was a smallish airedale, and it wagged the stump of its tail and wriggled its scrawny rump, ingratiatingly. Whitepaw responded by bringing into play every device for good-will in his nature, wriggling his way, meanwhile, to the pail, as the airedale picked up its bone and moved off with it.

Whitepaw then fell upon the pail, his muzzle dashing and darting to left and to right, like a thing apart from the rest of his body, pushing the pail around noisily in his efforts to get all there was in it, down his throat. Suddenly, he received a kick on his right hind leg which almost paralyzed him.

"Get out of here!" shouted a man.

Whitepaw leaped forward, sliding down the crust of the snow for nearly fifty feet. Whirling around a clump of bushtops, he raised his head and looked back. He saw a man moving about where the can had been spilled, saw him set the can upright and replace its cover.

When the man walked into the house, Whitepaw was afraid to go back, and his leg hurt him badly as he limped off to his niche under the bridge. It was hard for him to understand why a world which had always been so kind and generous to him, should have turned so cruel and hostile. But after a while he stopped licking at the bruise in his leg and closed his eyes with a sense of victory.

Unsatisfactory as his meal had been, painful as the bruise still was, he nevertheless had eaten. The thing to do about garbage pails was to be on guard as one ate from them. At any rate, there was food to be had in the frightful hubbub of city life; and while some city men were mean, not all the city dogs were vicious.

CHAPTER X

The Power of a Growl

AT DAYBREAK Whitepaw came out of his lair like a wolf, and stretched. Walking very slowly, still favoring the right hind leg, he went up the trail and sat down on the sidewalk, where the break in the ridge of snow enabled him to look into the street.

It was penetratingly cold and very hard to sit still. He had been driven away from his first meal in the city before he had been satisfied, but the fact that he had found food, there on that ledge, made sitting still, here on this cold sidewalk, unprofitable.

Yet here was where he had last seen Dwight; and every time something moved out in the street he looked up anxiously with renewed hope. But after scores of times in which the vehicles which announced their coming from the distance by the clanking of their chains, repeatedly turned out to be just more automobiles, instead of cutters drawn by horses, Whitepaw finally got up and again started down the slope.

He picked his way to a point from where he could see the shed where the garbage can had been, but the can did not seem to be there now. He made his way stealthily to the very spot, sniffed in the snow where it had stood, sniffed at the spot where the airedale had sat, chewing her bone. Suddenly the back door of the house opened, and he went tearing down the slope, and around the clump of bushtops.

A dozen times he returned to that shed, that day; and while he didn't find any food, each time that he sniffed the spot where the pail had stood, his hopes that he would find it revived.

Toward evening, snowflakes began falling from the grayish murk which had hung over the canyon all day long. The sharp-cut shadows in the ruts of the roadway filled up with white snow; and the slopes of the canyon began to look as if they had been washed clean. The iron bars of the bridge turned fat and soft, and the trolley cars going across dripped streaks of white snow dust, when they passed by. Houses stood out whiter, window lights oozed through cold, frosty lace, and the smoke from the chimneys was spattered with white sparks. Over the whole city hung a thick smell of burning soft coal, as if the falling snow was forcing it down to the ground.

That light in the side window was not the light in the teacher's house. He hadn't gotten over the brutal kick in his hind leg. But there had been food there, near that shed, and as the darkness began thickening enough to be protecting, he began making his way around the house again, and down the slope to the shed, exactly as he had done that first time.

It was more difficult to see clearly with the snowfall blurring things which the darkness failed to cover. There appeared to be no pail there yet, but the smell of food was there; and Whitepaw kept moving down. And there, to his delight, he spied the blurred form of the little airedale through the falling snow, working on something which he believed was the big pail.

Whitepaw eyed the back door of the house, even as he watched her. The little airedale seemed to know what she was doing. She diligently nudged the top of the pail with her bewhiskered muzzle. There was a stone on top of the cover, and as the airedale pushed, both of these went off into the snow. But the airedale continued pushing, until she had the pail over on its side and sent it rolling down the slope, halfway to the clump of bush-tops.

While the airedale stopped to pick up the food that had fallen out where she was, Whitepaw ran down the slope to the pail. When he looked back to make sure the man wasn't coming out again, the airedale was peacefully busy, and the flakes were falling gently.

Whitepaw gobbled up all that was eatable in and near the pail, then he began moving upward, along the trail which the thing had made, rolling down. As he moved up, eagerly grabbing at everything which looked as if it might be eaten, he was conscious of the fact that the airedale was doing the same thing, coming downward; and in his anxiety to get all he could before she had eaten everything up, he collided with her. She was apparently just as concerned about his taking what *she* wanted, but when they ran into each other, she rolled over on her side placatingly.

Whitepaw was hungry, but he had never been mean. He sniffed at her inoffensively and cordially wagged his big tail. The little airedale jumped up and affec-tionately licked his face; then she began leaping playfully around him, running off a short distance to show him that she wanted to play with him.

Whitepaw was delighted with her, but he was still hungry; and so he went on searching for more food in the snow. The airedale herself returned to the search; and they flitted around swiftly, here and there, their muzzles so low that they plowed the light surface of the newly fallen snow as they moved. In doing so, they came together upon the prize of the evening's find, a large joint bone.

Whitepaw had gotten hold of it, intending to carry it off a short distance; but when he dropped it to get a better grip, the airedale gracefully picked it up from under his lips, and started off with it.

There was no anger in Whitepaw, but the exasperation natural to the loss of a thing he wanted badly expressed itself in an unconscious growl. The effect of this instinctive threat was miraculous. The airedale dropped the bone and backed off respectfully.

Whitepaw picked it up, turned a few feet to the side; and lowering himself to the snow, went at gnawing it, losing himself completely in the pleasurable job. When his jaws began aching, and only half the bone was left, he looked up a moment, and found himself alone. Abandoning the hard piece of bone, he picked up the airedale's trail, and began searching for her. Her trail led him toward the bridge; and when he saw that familiar smear across the sky, with its sparkling, reddish lights gleaming in the snowfall, he decided to retire for the night.

He crept into his lair as if it belonged to him; and

he lay down to rest, this time, with a strange, cheerful sense of achievement. He was finding food and overcoming his hunger; and when he had growled, the airedale had stepped away from him, respectfully.

With all that, there was gnawing dissatisfaction in his heart, too. Time after time, he woke up from a dream of being with Dwight, in the teacher's house, about to reach for the plateful of good food Miss Martinby used to set before him, feeling her shoe under his muzzle, or the children petting him, in the school yard. Always on first awaking from such a dream, he would raise his head high with the impulse to race down the slope to the river and go tearing away back to the school yard; but he never moved out of the niche. He would merely lick his chops and curl up again. Up there in that break in the snow ridge along the sidewalk, he had seen Dwight last; and there he would see him again.

In the morning, Edmonton and the world was white with clean snow; and as Whitepaw sat himself down on the sidewalk to watch for the cutter and Dwight, his head kept turning to the right, and his eyes would look away up the long, narrow sidewalk for the collie. And his fear of the collie was softened by the memory of his miraculously effective growl, as the new-fallen snow had softened the harsh dirty lines of the city of the day before.

So many times, during that day, did he get the impulse to growl when he guarded against the approach of the collie, that in time he experienced a sort of disappointment because the collie wasn't coming; and late that night he got an unexpected opportunity to try his new-found power.

For some reason, the garbage pail did not appear that evening at the corner of the shed, on the ledge of the slope of the canyon. The little airedale was there on Whitepaw's second trip, and the two of them searched and went off, returning half a dozen times, without finding a trace of it. Nor were there any garbage pails at any of the other houses along the slope. The snow had stopped falling; and when the temperature dropped very low again Whitepaw preferred to roam the city searching for food to lying in his cold niche and shivering.

And because the airedale stayed with him, despite the stinging cold, Whitepaw enjoyed the endless trotting up and down the slope, from one ledge to another, around and around each house. They came, in the latter part of the night, to a row of houses on the canyon lip, half a mile to the east of the bridge. It was near daybreak. The milk deliveries had already been made in that part of the town. Whitepaw saw a bottle of milk on the porch, as he tripped around to the front of the first of the houses.

Suddenly remembering licking the top of one of these bottles, the night he had followed the bob sleigh, Whitepaw reached up to sniff at it. It had been extremely cold all night, and the cream in the upper part of the milk bottle had frozen and pushed the cap up, the frozen cream protruding for two inches above the bottle.

Whitepaw carefully licked it. The taste was so good, he bit into it, and the protruding cream broke off into his mouth. Slipping back down the porch steps with it, he lay down on the sidewalk to eat it. The airedale in the meantime, having watched him, went up on the porch to see what he had found there.

Suddenly the bottle came rolling down the steps, landing on the sidewalk with a crash. Immediately a window opened on the second floor of the house, and as Whitepaw slunk away, carrying a piece of the frozen cream in his mouth, he heard a woman's voice, angrily berating him. The airedale loped at his side, her mouth open as if she were laughing.

They fell back into a trot.

Out of reach of the angry voice, they fell back into a trot. The airedale, tripping along a few feet ahead, led him up on the sidewalk which ran along the edge of the canyon. Just as they came within sight of the blinking lights along the bridge, the airedale came to a sudden stop. Whitepaw saw the golden collie, as if he had just been unveiled in the darkness, hardly a dozen feet in front of them, standing in the middle of the sidewalk and watching them come.

They had all, at that point, come into the glow of a street light, and the darkness beyond the circle of light appeared like walls which would not let him get away. Whitepaw stopped dead still, frozen with fear, but he held his head fairly high, and through the center of him rumbled faintly a growl.

The collie stepped carefully and very slowly toward them, and the airedale went forward to meet him, wriggling coyly and wagging the stump of her tail.

The collie, head high, allowed the little airedale to lick his face and fuss over him, but he kept looking at Whitepaw, taking a step forward, growling threateningly.

Whitepaw didn't move, but the growl inside him rose into a roar. The little airedale took a look back at Whitepaw; then she went on as if she didn't care what they wanted to do; and to Whitepaw's surprise, the collie, pretending interest in the airedale, turned and trotted off after her.

Whitepaw remained standing frozen stiff, the growl inside him lowered, but continuing as if it were a mechanism that had gone wrong and couldn't stop. When the collie and the airedale were out of sight, he sprang over the ridge of snow and went down the slope.

At the river shore he turned westward to the bridge, and trotted up to his niche in the concrete base. He knew that his growl hadn't settled matters with the collie, as it had when he drove the airedale away from his bone, but he also knew that it had made the collie hesitate.

CHAPTER XI

Whitepaw Fights for Himself

THE teeming, noisy city looked different to White-paw, the following morning. No longer quite so much afraid of the golden collie, instead of remaining on the sidewalk he boldly stationed himself on a spot, on top of the ridge of snow, where he could see better. There, looking into the street where the automobiles would go by, from time to time, blowing the showers of churned-up snow into the air, he would sometimes forget what he was looking for, occasionally turning his head to the side to glance up the sidewalk, in the direction of the house from which the collie usually came.

When the automobiles which went slithering by came a bit too near to the snow ridge, Whitepaw would slip down to the sidewalk a moment, then climb up again when the car had passed.

One time, as he sat up there, he saw a black dog come out of a distant building and attack a passing machine, chasing it for a block, running along at its side and barking at it impudently. The automobile seemed to be running away from it, as if it were afraid. A hundred feet or so from where Whitepaw was sitting, the black dog gave up the chase, and tail proudly erect, it trotted off. Dog and automobile vanished, but as Whitepaw sat there looking on, every time a car came by he was half inclined to run at it and bark. At any rate, he ceased going down to the sidewalk.

By midafternoon, Whitepaw became weary sitting there and staring at cars, to no purpose. The temperature began dropping rapidly with the lowering of the sun, and so he started away. He had gone but a few steps westward when a man who was walking toward him stopped, and greeting him in a kindly voice, stroked his head and shoulders. The man went on eastward. Whitepaw looked after him hungrily, and hardly knowing what he was doing, he turned and walked after him.

The man was going in the direction of the house from which the collie always came, but his kindly voice and the touch of his hand pulled him along as with a rope. The man passed the house, and feeling queer, Whitepaw passed it too, close behind him. When they were a dozen feet on the other side, Whitepaw looked back. There was the golden collie on the sidewalk in front of the house, watching him.

Whitepaw felt the hair stiffen around his neck, and turning forward again and following the man, he growled with hatred. The man stopped and turning back to him said:

"What's the matter old fellow?"

Whitepaw wagged his tail and lowered his head, but the man petted him a moment and going on, Whitepaw continued to follow. A short distance farther east, a car came along the street, passed them a few feet and stopped. The car door opened, and the kind man jumped over the ridge of snow and got into it and drove away. Whitepaw stood there forlornly for several minutes, until the last black speck of the car disappeared in the distance. Even then, he couldn't give up following, trotting along eastward, and running up the ridge, every few yards, to look in the direction of the spot where the car had vanished.

He came to another group of houses along the canyon rim. A little poodle dog appeared on the porch of the first house and began barking in a frantic, high-pitched, silly little bark, which Whitepaw regarded as completely uncalled for. As soon as Whitepaw stopped to take a look at him, the little dog fled into the vestibule with a foolish *ki-yi*, as if he had bitten it. But while Whitepaw trotted on with nothing but contempt for his frenzy, the experience somehow made him feel very good.

A few blocks farther the sidewalk curved to the left, and there Whitepaw came to a succession of little stores. The air there was full of good smells coming from a butcher shop, a bakery, and a grocery store; but the doors of all were closed tight, and the big windows covered thick with frost. As Whitepaw moved along these, sniffing eagerly, hunger gnawing inside of him, he saw a bulldog working on a bone, in the middle of the sidewalk which led back to the grocery store.

Whitepaw stopped to stare at him enviously. As soon as the bulldog saw him, he got up with an angry look out of the sides of his rheumy eyes, seized his bone which was almost as big as *he* was, and lumbered off. Whitepaw followed him, a dozen feet behind. When the bulldog increased his pace Whitepaw increased his, keeping a sharp lookout against any other dog joining the chase.

The bulldog was half Whitepaw's size, but there was a determined and pugnacious look about the fellow, which kept Whitepaw at a respectable distance. The bulldog ran on, past the business section and on into a more sparsely settled district. Then, coming to the end of the block, the bulldog turned into the roadway to the middle of the street, and there, giving Whitepaw a wide berth, he turned back in the direction from which he had come.

Whitepaw got up on the snow ridge, at the edge of the sidewalk, and looked after him; and as he did so, he discovered a little girl coming up the sidewalk, walking along toward him, swinging a package in her mittened hands.

Little girls had always been noticeably gentler in the school yard than little boys; and as Whitepaw watched her coming, he was filled with a longing for the kindly touch of her warm little hand. But when he started eagerly toward her, he was surprised to see her hurry over the top of the ridge and into the street; and then, some distance past him, she ran back to the sidewalk. Still anxious to greet her, he trotted after her.

With a horrible shriek, the little girl started to run; and as she did so, she dropped her package. This seemed strange to Whitepaw, and he hesitated. Then noticing the package, he trotted up to it and sniffed.

It was meat! He was very hungry. Placing a paw upon the package, he tore away the paper with his teeth. He was so excited over this unexpected piece of good luck, that he forgot about the little girl. He was greedily trying to rip off a piece of the meat, when he saw in the twilight distance a woman coming out of a house and running to meet the little girl.

By this time, hungry as he was, he couldn't endure the thought of giving up the meat in his grasp; so, taking a firm grip on the package, he started up the ridge of snow on the canyon side of the sidewalk, and struck out for the river.

As he raced over the snow crust, he became aware of shouting voices, and he got the feeling that several people were coming after him. At the rim of the canyon, he looked back, and he could see them coming.

The slope was very steep there, and, accustomed now to sliding down the smooth, crusted incline, he let himself go toward a clump of bushes, a few feet up from the river shore. There he got to his feet quickly and whirled around to the other side of the bushes, from where he peered back up the incline. He saw two women, a man, and the little girl at the rim of the canyon, looking down. He crouched farther back behind the bushes; and then in the fading light, he saw them move along the rim a short distance and drop out of sight.

When they were gone, he looked carefully about in every direction. The canyon slopes and the river were motionless and completely deserted, the white stretches of snow crust dismally cold and lifeless. Pushing his way into the bushtops, backward so as to be safe from attack from the rear, he crouched down on his stomach, and until long after dark he lay there feasting.

By the time he had eaten away the three pound roast

from the huge bone in its center, Whitepaw felt that he had had enough. Remembering long hours of painful hunger, however, he wasn't going to throw away a good bone. He took it up carefully between his teeth, changing his hold several times before he had it so that it wouldn't impede his traveling, and started back home along the shore, pleased with himself and the world.

He followed the shore of the river, intending to bury his bone in the snow near his lair, where he could get it again when he was hungry. But just as he turned a curve in the river, from where he beheld the great bridge with its string of reddish lights, he saw a familiar little shadow, moving down the white slope toward him.

Whitepaw's big tail began to wag; and he stood there, the bone in his mouth, watching her make her way down to him. The little airedale was happy to come upon him, but her enthusiasm knew no bounds when she became aware of the bone in his mouth. Something in the way he was wagging his big tail made her feel that he wasn't going to growl at her; and so she sidled up to him, as he started off again, her shoulder pushing his shoulder, her muzzle reaching for the bone.

Whitepaw let her get hold of it, but he didn't let her have it; and as they ran along together, she led him diagonally up the slope. When they reached the edge of the canyon and the ridge of snow which lined the sidewalk, in the awkwardness of jumping over the mound of snow Whitepaw loosened his hold a moment. With a sudden pull and a deft turn, the airedale got the bone away from him.

Whitepaw didn't really care a great deal about her

taking that bone. He now enjoyed, however, displaying his strength. Heading her off as she was trying to lope away from him, he stood over her, head poised, and growled softly.

The little airedale dropped the bone and cringingly turned over on her side. Pleased with his success, Whitepaw was about to pick up the bone, when he saw the collie moving down upon him. Before he had time to turn, the collie clamped his jaws upon his shoulder, and Whitepaw felt the burning sting of his teeth, through his skin.

He tore himself loose and with blind fury and hatred hurled himself upon his tormentor, lashing out at him with more passion than sense.

The collie had more experience in fighting than Whitepaw had had. Everytime Whitepaw struck, he managed to spring away, pretending to run, only to whirl around and catch Whitepaw off guard. And suddenly the collie grabbed him by the throat.

Whitepaw knew at once that he had made a tragic mistake to let him get such a hold; but the more he tried to free himself, the tighter the collie gripped, creeping up in vicious jerks, gathering in between his murderous teeth, more and more of Whitepaw's throat.

That awful grip began choking off his breath. Things began to swim before his eyes; and he struggled desperately to keep from losing his balance. Then, into the confusion and fear in his addled brain came the cry of a man, and the thud of running feet.

Suddenly the vice on his burning throat fell away. Whitepaw heard angry voices, but it was hard for him

He clamped his teeth through fur and skin.

to see enough to get away. Blindly he crept over the ridge of snow slipping down a dozen feet or so, on the slope of the canyon. At a bunch of bushtops, he righted himself and looked back. No one was pursuing him. He saw nothing but white crust; and starting on down, he made his way painfully to the shore of the river.

By the time he came within the shadow of the bridge, he was quite himself again; but he sneaked up to his lair, more miserable than he had ever been in his life before. All the fears he had ever had seemed to have gathered together again, turning his life in the big city, to which he thought he had so successfully adjusted himself, into a nightmare, worse even than it had seemed to him that first awful evening when Dwight was swallowed up by the traffic on the street.

Even the niche in which he lay seemed safe no longer. The collie had come down that slope several times and now would come again. The very air and the snow seemed to smell strongly of him; and every strange little sound made him sit up and peer into the darkness.

The night was cruelly cold, stinging the open sores on his neck and shoulders; and it seemed endlessly long. And the morning brought him no relief. If anything, he was more afraid now than when the darkness had covered him. But he couldn't endure remaining in that niche after a long night of it. Several times he sneaked up to the sidewalk, but while he always went up there with the intense hope that this time he might see Dwight, he spent most of the time looking in the direction of the house where the collie lived.

By noontime, the collie having failed to appear,

Whitepaw had gotten over his intense fear of him, slightly, and once more began watching for Dwight. It was while he was peering into an unusual mass of traffic, that he suddenly turned and saw the collie coming full speed at him.

Whitepaw turned at once and shamelessly leaped into the cleft in the canyon rim and down the trail toward the bridge. But the collie had anticipated that move and turning at once and leaping over the ridge of snow, he slid down the crust on the slope, heading Whitepaw off just before he could plunge into the shadows under the bridge.

Whitepaw stopped. There seemed to be no use in trying now to evade the vicious dog. Horribly afraid of another grip upon his throat, he lowered his muzzle and expressed his fear and hatred in a growl that made him vibrate from head to foot.

The collie hesitated as if awed by that threat, and cautiously moved in a semicircle, trying to get at Whitepaw from the more advantageous rear.

This was a matter of life and death to Whitepaw, and he moved with the collie, every faculty alive to the danger. Then suddenly, the bitter resentment in his heart welling up in a maddening flood, he hurled himself recklessly upon his enemy. First he seized his shoulder, but as the big collie shook himself, Whitepaw's hold slipped. It slipped, but he wouldn't let go and in his blind determination, he got the entire legbone between his teeth.

The collie shook himself more violently, but so great was Whitepaw's fear of losing that hold that he clamped his teeth through fur and skin and drew blood. The collie shook himself even more violently, but because Whitepaw was determined not to let go, the collie lost his balance and went over on his side with a sharp little whimper of fear.

Had Whitepaw been a killer, he would have taken advantage of this, and would have switched his grip swiftly to the collie's throat. But Whitepaw only poured his remaining strength into his grip on the collie's leg, until he felt the bone crunch between his teeth, and heard the collie cry out in agony.

For a moment the surprise of the collie's yelp startled Whitepaw, and he experienced the illusion of something or someone else coming into the bewildering scene. He let go his hold and looked up, but though there was no one there on the deserted white snows, and the collie managed to right himself and limp away, Whitepaw made no move to get hold of him again.

He stood there watching him limp, for a few seconds, then he trotted after him, leisurely, remaining a few feet behind him. Up on the sidewalk, Whitepaw sat down and watched the collie stagger off toward the house where he lived. He licked his chops with satisfaction, even as he still panted for breath. He knew that the collie would not soon be back to torment him again.

CHAPTER XII

No Limitations to Hunger

IN SPITE of his victory over the golden collie, Whitepaw guarded the direction in which the collie lived with untiring care. While his eyes glared shiningly at the point where he always expected to see the collie coming, his tongue would lash out over his muzzle with determination, and in his teeth he would feel the strange, passionate urge to crunch with all his strength. When several days went by without any signs of the collie, he began moving about his post with an unquestioned air of possession.

At the same time, the urgent business of searching for something to eat made it necessary to keep cutting down the number of daylight hours of watching for Dwight. He never let a whole day go by, however, without sitting on that cold sidewalk for some time, looking into the endless motion of traffic.

As people resented having their garbage scattered over their yards, garbage pails ceased to appear. And those who were displeased by Whitepaw's eating the frozen cream off their milk bottles had their milk left where he could not get at it.

He began to feel that people were watching for him, in dark corners, and he acquired the cunning not to go back to the same house on two successive nights. The love he used to feel for all human beings seemed to have turned into the ingenuity of a cat regarding them. He began reaching out in his search for food to the farther districts of the city, keeping always within reach of the safety of the winding canyon. And as the winter was hard, and food scarce, he was driven to greater and greater desperation and boldness.

He came to a secluded little house on the outskirts of the city one cold night, shortly after his fight with the collie, where he ran into the scent of grouse. He hadn't forgotten the grouse which Dwight and he had eaten, the first few days after leaving the teacher's house. He picked up the scent as he was sniffing near the door of the woodshed which was attached to the rear of the house.

The door happened to be a flimsy one, full of cracks which oozed with the tantalizing grouse scent, and it gave slightly, as he pushed at it. But it gave only an inch at a time and made too much noise; and after allowing his head into the shed, it seemed to stop giving. The scent of grouse was now so intense, however, that he was not willing to give up and go away. He discovered that by rising up on his hind legs, he could reach a place in the door where it was springy and gave several inches farther. Through that part of the opening, between door and doorframe, he leaped in.

Once inside, he sat down to rest a bit, and to look about and sniff carefully. In the extremely dim light which came from the frost-covered window at the side of the door, he made out layers of stove wood against the wall to his right; while against the opposite wall, he

saw a long table. The scent of grouse came from the
table side of the shed; and soon, as he peered eagerly in
the darkness, he made out the birds, a whole row of
them, hanging on nails on the wall, over the table.

He sprang up, on to the table, and there, getting on
his hind legs, he reached for the nearest of the birds,
seizing it by the neck which hung down. But the tied
legs wouldn't come off the nail higher up, and when
he pulled a bit too eagerly, he lost his balance. Down
he went, and something on the table went crashing
down with him. In his haste to get to the door, his shoulder struck one of the layers of wood and half the wood
against the wall went clattering to the floor.

When he tried to get out through the small opening
between the door and its frame, his shoulder pulled it to,
against his neck; and before he could back out again, he
heard steps in the house. The door of the house opened
into the shed with a flood of light, and a voice cried:
"Get out of here!"

Whitepaw caught a glimpse of an apparition—a man
in a long white nightgown, a kerosene lamp in his hand;
but he didn't stop to look at it. He tried to get out of
the narrow opening again, but he had barely pushed his
head through, when he received a blow on the rump
that almost paralyzed him.

Infuriated, he pulled back to defend himself, as he
had learned to defend himself; but as he turned to face
the man, another stick hit him on the head, a third
struck the door and a fourth crashed through the window to the side of the door.

As he sprung toward the man, the fellow let out a

horrible shriek, and the lamp dropped from his hand with a crash. Instantly a flame shot up into the air, almost shutting the man off from his view.

Whitepaw had had his experiences with fire, and he had no desire to experiment with it. Now he had but one thought and that to get out, as soon as possible. As

The fellow let out a horrible shriek.

he was about in his desperation to try the door again, something about the way in which the flames behind him reflected in the upper half of the window, but not in the lower half, made him realize that the lower half had been broken out.

In one jump, he leaped through the broken window, and with the fire light playing nervously on the snow crust, he made for the canyon as straight and as fast as he could go, vaguely expecting pieces of wood to hit him as he ran. When he got to the very edge of the canyon, he turned to look back. Flames were now visible through the broken window and the narrow opening in the door; and a man, coming from a nearby house, broke across the red light, and began pushing his way in through the door.

There were too many troublesome possibilities in these people, and this fire, for Whitepaw to care to stay there and look on. Down the slope of the canyon, he went, slinking nervously from bush to bush, stopping at each to look back, but continuing to get farther and farther away, though no one appeared to be running after him.

There was no doubt in his mind about his having done something that was severely punishable. And even though no one was pursuing him, he had the vague feeling that they would be seeking him. So strong was this feeling that he was afraid to go back to his lair in the concrete base of the bridge support, and he struck out across the frozen river.

On the other side of the river, he looked back and seeing the light of the fire still blazing beyond the opposite rim of the canyon, he zigzagged up the other slope, making his way from one bush to another, getting behind each of them and looking back, before he ventured on up farther.

On the open flats above, with all the canyon and the river between him and the fire he had started, he sat down more leisurely and gazed at the flickering red light, which was now too far away to worry him a great deal. Soon tiring of that, he started westward, vaguely feeling in his mind that he would get back to the bridge, going that way, and that in getting back to his lair from that side, the men would not be able to pick up his scent.

He came to a small, scattered group of houses at the outskirts of Strathcona, the town which is on the opposite side of the Saskatchewan River from Edmonton. Each little house seemed to have its own little barn, and everything was half-covered with snow. Most of the houses were dark and silent and motionless.

Between the first of these little houses and its squatty barn, was a woodpile. As no dog appeared to be living at that house, and the people were either asleep or gone out, Whitepaw stopped to sniff in the hope that he might find something to eat.

There wasn't anything around the back of the house, where he usually found things to eat; but as he started to leave, he passed the woodpile where he found a chicken head near the chopping block. It wasn't the best sort of food, according to Whitepaw's bringing up, but it was cold and he needed meat and he was hungry enough to eat anything. He picked it up and trotting off to a safe open space, away from the house, he sat down and ate it.

He had intended going back to the woodpile to search for another chicken head, sure that there must be more there, but suddenly he became aware of a man crunching the hard, cold snow in the distance, coming unmistakably toward that little house, and so he got up and slunk away, hitting the nearest sidewalk and following it into the thicker section of Strathcona. There he turned northward toward the canyon, went down the snow-crusted canyon slope, crossing the frozen river diagonally, and picking his way cautiously to his niche in the concrete base, under the bridge.

Most of the following morning he slept in his lair, and during the slightly warmer afternoon he sat on the sidewalk and watched for Dwight, wagging his tail when an occasional passer-by stopped to say a kind word to him, but carefully keeping aloof, ready to flee if need be.

As soon as it grew dark enough to hunt with any kind of safety, Whitepaw trotted down to the river, crossed to the other side, now, and climbing up the south slope to the flats above, headed straight for the sparsely settled east end of Strathcona and the tiny farm where he had found the chicken head.

He went directly to the woodpile, keeping his eyes cautiously on the faint light which trickled from a small window in the side of the house. He didn't find another chicken head at the chopping block, as he had expected to, but there were many tracks of chickens in the snow, going off from the woodpile, in several directions. The one he picked out to follow, led right by the little window in the side of the house and off to the squatty little barn, a hundred and fifty feet away.

The trail led him to the barn door where the snow was stippled with chicken tracks. The little barn, as was the entire farmyard, was shrunken by the extreme coldness into the general stillness of the winter night. Nothing seemed to be stirring anywhere. Emboldened by the secluded quietness, Whitepaw tried to push open the barn door, but this door did not give in the least.

When he shoved his muzzle tight against the crack between the door and its frame, the smell of chicken was
so strong that it made his mouth water.

The little barn faced the south, its rear receiving the
brunt of the snow-laden winter winds from the north.
Up against its north side, there was a huge drift which
sloped to within a foot of its straw-thatched roof. Going around the squatty little building, Whitepaw climbed
the drift, intending merely to search completely around
the barn for some possibly easier opening. But at the
highest point of the drift, under the overhanging straw,
he caught sight of a small, dark object.

He stopped dead still in his tracks. It was a chicken,
somehow left out that evening, when the rest of the
chickens had been driven into the coop for the night.
It was standing on one leg, half-frozen, dozing. Looking hastily about, Whitepaw slipped up to it and seized
it by the neck.

He was very nervous when he turned with this big
thing dangling from his jaws, and no little worried; and
in his worry was the fear that he might lose it. He
clamped his jaws together, tighter and tighter, with
something of the passion with which he had crunched
the leg-bone of the golden collie; and he twisted the
thing unwittingly as he kept whirling around from one
side to the other, to make sure that the owner of the
little farm wasn't coming out after him. When at last,
he dropped the thing, half a mile away, on the open
snows near the edge of the canyon, there wasn't a trace
of life left in it. For a while he sat there, panting for
breath and looking about, then picking it up again, he

carried it to a bush-top, sticking out of the hard crust, and there he lay down to feast.

He was getting fairly well filled up, when as he looked back toward the distant coop and the house beside it, he saw the familiar little shadow of the airedale, moving swiftly over the white crust, down the drift. Somewhere she had picked up his trail and had followed it unerringly to the coop.

At first, his wild instincts revived, Whitepaw seized what was left and holding his muzzle down to the snow with it, growled threateningly. With a hurt look on her square-jawed head, the airedale sat down a few feet away and licked her chops. Whitepaw watched her through the sides of his eyes, as he slowly returned to his eating; then abruptly he relented, and began wagging his tail.

The little airedale became happily active. She got up and wriggled ingratiatingly, venturing nearer and nearer. Finally, she reached in beside his muzzle, carefully took hold of a morsel of the meat and began to pull it. Whitepaw was not used to this kind of fare. The entire theft of the hen and his tearing it apart were something very new to him. As soon as his hunger had been somewhat satisfied, the whole business satiated him. The airedale found plenty to eat, and Whitepaw let her eat. And while she was busy, he trotted all around the snows, rubbing his muzzle sideways, on the snow crust, first on one side then on the other, rolling over on his back and kicking his legs in the air. The airedale was still trying to salvage some piece of bone or skin from the mess of feathers before her, when Whitepaw began plaguing her, running around her, nipping her, pretending to bite her, throwing her over.

They began playing over the hard crusts of the snow, running as fast as they could in wide, crazy circles, and in that manner they played until dawn, as dogs barked at them, in the distance, pawing each other, pretending to bite, rolling over each other, finally chasing each other toward the canyon, down the slope and across the river.

For two nights Whitepaw kept away from that section of the canyon, going back to his earlier discoveries, the houses on the ledge west of the bridge and those along the north rim of the canyon. But the garbage pails he had pillaged did not reappear, and the milk bottles were put safely out of his reach.

The third night, after his experience with the chicken, Whitepaw was so hungry again that visions of chickens standing on the drift began to haunt him; and once more he picked his way to the east end of Strathcona.

He was very much disappointed not to find another hen on the drift, waiting for his arrival; and he trotted around and around the little coop, sniffing every crack and corner for some way of getting into it. The door was impossible, and after every attempt to scratch it open with his paws, he went back to the top of the drift in back, with renewed hope. Each time that he sniffed the spot where the unfortunate hen had stood on one leg, he also sniffed the tar-papered wall, all the way up to the overhanging thatch. And each time he touched the thatch he pushed it a little harder with his nose. Then one time, as he did so, there blew into his face a warm waft of air, reeking with the smell of the chickens inside.

Whitepaw became very much excited, pushing at the straw with more and more energy. As the straw appeared to be quite loose, he bit into it, tearing out a tuft of it. When he threw the straw out of his mouth and sniffed where he had bitten, there was a small hole there, from which the warm, chicken-smelling air poured out in a stream.

Suddenly, Whitepaw heard a soft patter on the snow. He was inclined to believe that it was the airedale coming, but he took no chances. Slipping swiftly down the other side of the drift, he stopped at a safe distance and looked back. When he saw her looking down at him, obviously puzzled by his flight, he trotted back to her.

The airedale watched him tearing straw from the roof with delight and soon joined in the sport. Soon they had a hole big enough for one of them to go through. Whitepaw got up on the roof and standing with his forefeet over the hole, he lowered his head slowly into it. Hurriedly sniffing around in there, he located a row of chickens, pressed close together on the topmost roost, about a foot below the straw roof. As he carefully reached down, clinging to the roof with his forepaws, afraid that he might lose his balance, there came a drowsy *purp-purping* from the sleepy chicken heads, all along the row, protesting against the coldness let in by the hole.

He was a bit too anxious and much too nervous, and in his effort to grab one of the heads, he knocked that chicken off the roost. The falling hen sent out a cry of alarm; and the one next to her spread her wings to regain her balance. Whitepaw closed his jaws upon one of these wings.

The hen set up a raucous noise which was taken up by several of the rest of the chickens; but Whitepaw jerked it clear out of the hole and leaped down to the drift top. In doing so, he lost his hold on the hen and the thing started to run, sending its cries to high heaven. The airedale who had been tripping around nervously, caught it before it could get away. Whitepaw tore the hen out of the airedale's grasp, as he heard a door slam.

This time he had a good hold on the creature's neck, so that it no longer squawked, but the thing was so big that it dangled at his feet and dragged on the snow every time he turned his head to look back.

By the time the farmer had gone into the coop and made his investigation without discovering the hole in the roof, Whitepaw and the airedale had reached the canyon and were safely on their way down to the river.

Near some bushes on the river shore, he dropped the thing, and it lay perfectly still. Panting for breath, Whitepaw looked carefully about him and back up the slope, but while there was no sign of anyone coming after him, he didn't feel quite safe yet. Picking up his loot again, he trotted away, the airedale eagerly tripping along his side. As they turned with a bend in the river and the canyon, Whitepaw saw in the distance the big black smear of the bridge, its reddish, star-like lights blinking high over the river ice. There, near a bush, they stopped to eat.

It was still quite early in the night, when they were through with their savage meal; but being unusually full, Whitepaw wanted to go back to his lair and lie down. It was very cold that night, and so he tried to induce the airedale to go to his niche with him. Every time she left the direct route to his lair, he leaped in front of her and headed her off; but when they got to within a quarter of a mile of the bridge, she got away from him and raced up the incline.

Whitepaw followed her, thinking that he would turn her down again, but as they reached the house where the collie lived, the fellow leaped off the porch as if he had been waiting for him.

He stopped a few feet from Whitepaw, and as he stiffened up, seeming to inflate himself to a greater height, he began to growl deep down his throat. Whitepaw was a different dog from the one who used to run from him; but at the moment, he was still thinking of detaining the little airedale. In the time that he took to glance at her, because she was trotting away, the collie jumped for his throat.

The long-coming, last struggle was on as with one mind. Each dog wisely guarding his throat, striking and leaping back, tripping around in a semicircle on the sidewalk, to seek an advantage and to guard against giving one, the snarling and the growling rose louder and louder like the crackle of a fire that was spreading and going out of bounds.

Whitepaw early realized that the collie would not willingly let him get a hold on his throat. Remembering his first victory over his red enemy, Whitepaw tried to get another of his legs between his teeth, but apparently the collie remembered it too. Because Whitepaw was obsessed by the passion to get hold of the collie's leg, he was not guarding his own body as well as he might. He felt burning sensations in both shoulders and on one side of his mouth, where the collie had ripped it, aiming at his throat. But these hurts only inflamed Whitepaw's passion to get hold of a leg.

They moved around like fighting roosters, up the sidewalk and down the sidewalk, over one ridge of snow and over the other and back again to the sidewalk; and then suddenly Whitepaw got his chance. He closed his teeth upon the collie's right leg with such a snap that he penetrated his hide at once. And then immediately, with blind and almost insane hatred, he jerked the collie off balance, even as he crushed the bone in his jaws.

The collie let out a siren-like series of yelps of agony. Whitepaw had him now where he could do what he wanted with him. Throwing him over on his back by deftly wrenching the leg in his mouth, he was about to drop the leg and go for his throat, when he received a whack on his rump that sent an electric shock through his body. For a second he was on the verge of yelping for pain himself. Then as things cleared in his befuddled brain sufficiently to make him realize that he had been struck by a man, his anger exploded, seemingly lifting him into the air. He whirled upon the man behind him, just as the stick was about to come down upon him again, his jaws snapping upon the lifted arm, with the speed with which he had learned to catch snowballs in the schoolyard.

The man let out a frightened yell for help. The yell sobered Whitepaw. Letting go of the arm, he turned, sprang clear across the snow ridge, whisked into the shadows of the house and down the slope of the canyon.

As he slid down the slippery snow crusts, he heard men running on the sidewalk, and he slunk fearfully into the shadows under the bridge.

In his niche, he lay licking his wounds, his ears pricked high. Even when the night settled down again cold and still, he remained worried. It was not natural to grapple with a *man*.

THE NEXT morning, people of Edmonton read the following article in the Edmonton Daily Register, the third in a series written by George Harding, the publisher's son, on the doings of the mysterious wild dog who had been pillaging several sections of the town, night after night:—

MYSTERIOUS WILD DOG CONTINUES TO PLAGUE CITY'S RESIDENTS.

CANINE DR. JEKYLL AND MR. HYDE PUZZLES POLICE.

Police Chief Harold Simmons is of the opinion that the mysterious wild dog who has been stealing milk from porches, frightening children on their way from the store and taking their food away from them, will prove to be a sort of Dr. Jekyll and Mr. Hyde of the canine world, who sits at his beloved mistress's feet by day and turns into a veritable devil by night.

Several nights ago he was reported to have knocked the lamp out of the hands of Sam Gleason, out in Brevier district, setting his woodshed afire. Last night he attacked the prize collie of the Palmers', on River Street; and when Mr. Palmer attempted to rescue his dog the beast leaped for this throat. Only his presence of mind and the stick with which he had supplied himself saved his life, he avers.

Weird stories of the dog's uncanny cleverness keep coming into the police, many of which the police are inclined to discount. Nevertheless, Chief Simmons is making elaborate plans for the capture of the culprit. So long is the list of damages piling up against the marauder that the police are as anxious to find the dog's owner as they are to capture the dog.

CHAPTER XIII

Iron in Winter

LONG after the brassy sun had arisen, the following morning, Whitepaw continued to lie in his uncomfortable niche in the concrete base of the bridge support, very much inclined to go up to his watch post on the sidewalk above, but strangely hesitant about doing so. He hardly thought about the collie at all. He was superior to the collie now, and in his triumphant consciousness still rang out the siren-like yelping of the collie's expression of defeat.

But fighting and defeating the collie was one thing, and fighting and defeating the man was another—fundamentally different. It was not even that one offensive man alone. It was something that had to do with all men, something which would bring unthinkable punishment out of the mysterious and miraculous power of man to punish.

By noon, however, Whitepaw simply could not stay in his niche any longer. Cautiously he crept out of the shadows under the bridge into the snowy trail going up the incline; but the first time he saw a man walk by on the sidewalk above, he slipped back, ashamed, so that he would not be seen.

The cold dismal afternoon gave way to evening, and the waning gray day grew colder with each moment.

The extreme cold made it impossible for him to sit still. It made it just as impossible to lie in his stony niche; and the aches and hurts all over him made it almost as disagreeable to move about.

When the early darkness of the long winter night came down, Whitepaw meandered around the slopes of the canyon and the river shore, looking everywhere, sniffing everything, seeking what, he hardly knew, finding nothing. Tormented by his hurts and his aches, his loneliness was more heavy upon him than his hunger, and as he searched aimlessly the image of the little airedale came more and more poignantly into his seeking.

The intense cold made the snow shrink into dry powder which complained even as the pads of his feet ground it over the icier crusts; and his breath rose from his muzzle like smoke, as he moved aimlessly from place to place, finding it too cold to sit down.

He started finally toward the houses along the ledge on the wall of the canyon, where he had first come upon the airedale. The light was there in the window of that house, as it had been that first night. He sat down and studied it a moment. It suggested again the teacher's house in the schoolyard, and again a deep hunger for the life that had been snatched away from him filled him. He got up and trotted off around the house, exactly as he had done that first night. He slid past the frost-covered window, and down along the other wall of the house, to the corner from where he could see the dark shed along the back, half expecting to see the little airedale, turning over the big garbage can, and rolling it down the slope.

The airedale was not there, but the garbage pail was out again, standing against the wall of the shed. Whitepaw forgot about the airedale for the moment and hungrily stole up to the side of the pail with its iron top and the stone upon it. Like an expert, Whitepaw pushed up at the iron cover, but he sprang back in fright. The thing had stung his nose, burning it like fire.

He looked over to the house. The door was shut tight. He lifted a paw and brushed his nose, which in the extreme cold, felt as if something were clinging to it. It pained him badly and he was nervous and afraid; but he was hungry, and in the shriveling cold, hunger was more serious than in normal weather. It seemed impossible for him to go away and leave the food that he could now smell in the can.

He moved back toward the thing very carefully, a few inches at a time, stopping from time to time and looking toward the house and sniffing the biting air. At the garbage pail he sniffed carefully all around, to learn whether there was something there which might hurt him; but all he could smell with the food odors was the pungent odor of iron. He knew that iron smell and merely accepted it as the iron cover, which he would have to push away to get into the pail.

But when at last he pushed at the cover with his nose again, the iron stuck to his tender skin, where it had merely burned it before. As he sprang back with a cry of pain, he pulled the whole thing over, stone, pail and cover.

The contents of the pail were now clearly exposed,

but Whitepaw was afraid to go near it. There had been no school to teach him that when temperature goes down low, iron will stick to a moist nose—no school but this hard one of experience. And the school of experience offers no mere passable marks for half learning. A hundred percent hurt, and Whitepaw learned. His nose burned as if it were on fire, and he fled to his lair, where he lay most of the night, promising himself to keep away from iron-covered garbage pails.

Shortly before dawn, unable to endure the excruciating cold without stirring, he made his way up to the sidewalk above the canyon rim. The city lights up there blinked sleepily, but the traffic had vanished. The street with its many automobile tracks in the snow was completely deserted.

Whitepaw looked up the sidewalk, forlornly. There was nothing to go to, nothing to go for. But there was nothing for him there on that sidewalk either. He turned his head wearily and looked across where the traffic had swallowed up the cutter with Dwight. He hesitated about going off in that direction, for it would take him away from the canyon, where his safety lay. As he looked back up the empty sidewalk, it occurred to him that he might go on eastward to the houses on the other side of the house where the collie lived, and see whether someone might not have set a milk bottle down on one of the porches. Unwilling to risk a fight with the collie while his nose was so sore, he went down to the river and eastward along the shore, till he had passed beyond the collie's house, then turned back up the slope to the sidewalk.

There, he looked about him again. Wherever he looked there was not a living, moving thing to be seen. Every house was shrunk within itself, dark and lifeless, many of its outlines wiped out by the whiteness of streaks of snow, and all the windows, everywhere, were thick with frost.

From one of these houses to the other, he slunk along, stopping here and there, lifting his muzzle half-heartedly and sniffing from the distance. There were no milk bottles out on a night like this; and every door that could shut, was shut forbiddingly tight.

From street to street, Whitepaw tripped along, hopelessly, hungrily, the breath rising from his painful muzzle, his ghostly shadow grayed on the white surface of the snows, until dawn came over the housetops and traffic poured life into the street. And when the sun appeared, he found his favorite sunny spot near the sidewalk, and lay down to sleep.

The days were so short, now, hardly had Whitepaw warmed a bit of life into his body, when the feeling of evening began creeping back into the air. So long as there was any daylight left in the atmosphere, Whitepaw fidgeted on the cold sidewalk; but as soon as the night came down, he started for the little coop at the east end of Strathcona.

Twice in succession, Whitepaw had found a hen at that little chicken coop which was full of such hens. And as he trotted along, in his business-like manner, he imagined himself getting up on that straw roof, dipping down through the hole, and pulling out another meal.

He raced up the shore without doubt or hesitation.

He knew just the right point from which to strike out diagonally across the frozen river. He climbed up the south wall of the canyon, almost in the very tracks he had himself made in the snow, and hit out across the open crusts on the flats above to the long drift, up to the thatched roof of the coop.

The frozen winter world was so still and lifeless, that Whitepaw trotted right up to the roof before he thought it necessary to stop and take his usual, precautionary measures. When he listened, he could hear no sounds. But when he sniffed near the hole in the straw, he got the feeling this secret of his had been tampered with. He became extremely suspicious. As he studied things carefully, he noticed a piece of iron protruding from the hole, a few inches beyond the edge of the roof.

He didn't know, of course, that a badger trap had been set for him. In fact, he didn't know that there was such a thing as a trap in the world. But he knew, now, that iron can hurt badly, these cold, wintry nights; and he wasn't going to take any chances with iron.

To avoid the piece of iron which he had sniffed from the snow drift, he got up on the roof and at the hole, from its upper edge. But there was iron up there, too, and he quickly leaped down to the drift again. Moving off a few feet, to the side, he began to tear out the straw with the idea of making another hole in the roof.

But as he spat out his first mouthful of straw, he was surprised by a very fine wire which caught in his teeth; and because it didn't fall right out and he was frightened, he pulled back so hard that he broke it. He had pulled back with the idea of getting away from there as soon as he could, but when nothing hurtful followed the breaking of the wire, being ravenously hungry, he crept back cautiously to try again.

Suddenly he heard the little house door open, and as he turned, he saw a long stream of light which shot past the right side of the coop and set the snow crust afire to the very edge of the canyon.

For several seconds he couldn't move at all, then he started tremblingly down the long drift. By the time he got to the end of the drift, the light which was hurting his eyes, seemed to turn around him like a hook and shut off his escape to the canyon.

Whitepaw swerved to his left and raced toward the heart of Strathcona. As he raced wildly, he was bewildered by the play of several lights, and turning around to see what was happening, he saw two motorcycles and what seemed like two men mounting them. He was not sure whether they were really coming after him, but he didn't wait to find out. Westward now, he leaped like a jackrabbit.

Over hummocks, down through hard, snow-crusted hollows he galloped, avoiding houses and barking dogs; then he hit a long stretch of well-swept sidewalk. A bit reassured about the chance to make distance on that sidewalk, he stopped for a second to look back once more. Sure enough, the motorcycles were right behind him.

In front of him was a brightly lighted house, and a big brown dog on the porch was looking at him with a great deal of obvious interest. Whitepaw turned away from him, leaping over the ridge of snow along the sidewalk and into the middle of the snow-plowed street, but before he got to the next intersection, the motorcycle which was nearest to him caught up to him, went on a few yards ahead and turned.

Now Whitepaw was sure that the motorcycle men were after him. Turning back toward the houses, he hopped over both of the snow ridges along the sidewalk, and plunged into the dark spaces between the two houses in front of him. When beyond them he broke out into the next street, he saw the second motorcycle bearing down upon him. Again he turned westward, but as soon as he reached the next avenue, he could hear and almost feel the two motorcycles coming together upon him from both sides.

The fact that the motorcycles clung to the plowed part of the road in the street, made him feel safer in the darkened spaces between houses, where he felt they couldn't follow him very well.

Block after block he ran breathlessly, clinging to sides of houses and sheds, galloping across well-lighted spaces, and ducking into shadows along hedges and fences wherever he could, hearing and feeling the motorcycles on the streets, both sides of him, so tired now that he felt the weight of his body dragging him down to the snow.

When he came to the wide, main avenue of the town, which led to and over the bridge to Edmonton, both motorcycles came together again within a few inches of his tail. But worn out though he was, going more and more slowly all the time, he managed to escape them, although as he ran, he expected at any moment to have to drop in his tracks.

He came to a wide open street where he saw to the side of him the dark cluster of the University of Alberta buildings. Directly in front of him was the campus; and even though he still heard the motorcycles, he struck out diagonally over the snow crust, between the trees. Before he got to the middle of the campus square, both motorcycle lights picked him out between the trees and exposed him. To the side of him was a long, high hedge, sticking up several feet above the deep snows, and he plunged into its shadow.

Closer to the hedge, he discovered an opening and slipping through it, he came out into a small street, leading southward. It was a quiet little residential street, and though most of the frost-covered windows were glowing with light, the street itself was shrouded in peaceful darkness.

He walked heavily across the roadway, his body now too much for his worn-out legs, and as he hit the sidewalk he heard the motorcycles coming around the two corners behind him. The sound of the motorcycles goaded him into a slightly faster trot, but his frightened eyes searched the dark spaces around him for some place in which to hide.

He lowered his muzzle for the merest flash of a moment to sniff toward a break in a snow-buried wicket fence, when he suddenly picked up a scent on the sidewalk which electrified him.

The motorcycles were now right behind him, but even the terror of their nearness could not swerve his muzzle from that scent. His nose to the sidewalk, he forged ahead breathlessly, turning with it through a tiny gateway. Following the scent along the center of a narrow little sidewalk, he leaped up the three steps of the porch. Near the door, the porch floor was reeking with the scent of Dwight's boots, and he fell upon the door, lifting himself to his full height. There, scratching at the crack with his claws, Whitepaw barked and barked and barked.

The porch floor was reeking with the scent of Dwight's boots.

CHAPTER XIV

Paying Damages

DWIGHT was sitting forlornly on the edge of the well-cushioned davenport, in the cozy little parlor of Miss Martinby's home, his face in his hands, his elbows on his knees. His wrinkled forehead was pale and his hollow cheeks still showed the effects of his illness, despite Miss Martinby's generous feeding and care, since he had left the hospital.

Miss Martinby, on the davenport with him, was talking with John Burnell, who was sitting on a rocker facing them. In a corner of the delightfully warm room, at an old-fashioned mahogany secretary, Miss Martinby's mother, a woman in her seventies, was apparently writing a letter. The old lady looked up at the farmer, abruptly, with an expression of displeasure on her wrinkled, kindly face.

"Dr. Andrews says y'u'll jes' have t' go back home with me," John Burnell was saying. "Now that the dog's grown big, Dr. Andrews says that maybe I had ought t' let y'u bring 'im home with y'u. I shouldn't give in. I'll let y'u have y'ur way this time, Dwight; but y'u ain't goin' t' have y'ur way like that any more, an' don't y'u forget that."

The old lady in the corner turned back to her writing. It was evident that she had found it hard to hold back some of the things she had had on the tip of her tongue to say to the farmer. John Burnell, however, completely missed her critical glance. He was waiting for Dwight to answer, but the boy hardly moved.

"I got t' take that 'leven o'clock train," the farmer went on, resentfully. "I can't sit around here waitin' for the dog t' show up. The Missus is home alone, doin' all the chores herself—bad cold spell like this."

"I don't want to go back," muttered Dwight under his breath.

John Burnell pretended not to have heard that.

"The natural thing for that dog t' do," he began with a new line of attack, "is t' go right back where he come from. Dogs'll find their way back to their homes, hundreds of miles away. I'll bet y'u a nickel that durn fool dog's back there in the schoolyard right now, awaitin' f'r y'u t' come an' feed 'im."

Dwight looked up, startled. He had heard before that dogs have been known to travel many miles to get back to homes from which they had been taken. The idea that Whitepaw might at this moment be starving or freezing in the deserted schoolyard, horrified him.

"I saw him right behind the cutter," he blurted out, as if arguing with himself. "I turned and looked around when we come up from the river into the street, an' he kep' right behind us."

"I got work t' do at home," repeated the farmer, stirring angrily in his rocker. "This is all a lot o' foolishness."

"Why don't you let Dwight stay here a few days longer?" suggested Miss Martinby. "He will feel stronger by that time, and he can take the train alone. By tomorrow, if the cold lets up a little, we'll let him go out looking for the dog along the river. On the other hand, if when you get back to Vermillion, you should find Whitepaw there at the school, you could write and let us know."

A look of painful doubt came over Dwight's face. The idea of leaving this cozy, kindly home and going back to the Burnell farm was not a happy one. At the same time, if Whitepaw had really gone back to the schoolyard, he preferred, of course, to go back with Burnell, at once. He was not at all willing to trust the farmer with Whitepaw, even for a few days. The dog might be half-starved by this time. He sat up and gazed intently at the farmer, trying to find the words with which to express himself, but the old lady spoke up from her corner at the desk.

"What do you intend to do about the hospital bill, Mr. Burnell?" she asked.

"When I explained the circumstances to the hospital supervisor," put in Miss Martinby, "she reduced the bill to forty-eight dollars, exactly half of what it should have been."

John Burnell glared angrily at the boy.

"There is also another bill that will have to be paid," Miss Martinby continued. "Dwight became very sick, trudging through the snows in the blizzard. He was obliged to break into Harry Lorwell's hunting lodge to save his life. He had to stay there several days. He used up quite a little of Lorwell's supplies of food and fuel, and that will be at least ten dollars more to pay for."

"You're the one, Miss Martinby, that had ought t' pay the whole business," growled the farmer angrily. "You put the runnin' away idea into the kid's head."

"I want t' pay it all myself," began Dwight, uncertainly; but they apparently did not consider him in the discussion at all.

"I can't understand how you can say such a thing," said Miss Martinby with a visible effort to be patient.

"Y'u give 'im y'ur address, didn't y'u?" cried Burnell. "Why'd y'u give 'im y'ur address, if y'u wasn't thinkin' of his runnin' away?"

"That's nonsense," replied Miss Martinby. "I wanted him to write to me. I think Dwight is a very fine boy whom you do not understand. He was so unhappy and discouraged at your place, I wanted to help him. I thought I might outline some studying for him, if you people should be unable to get a teacher, next year."

"If you had tried a little to make the boy happy," said the old lady, "maybe he wouldn't have wanted to run away."

"He was all right till y'ur daughter put ideas int' his head."

"She was hired to put ideas into his head," retorted Mrs. Martinby, turning about in her chair and facing the farmer belligerently. "But that's getting away from the point. The point is that if you insist on his going back because Dr. Andrews has put him in your care, you will have to pay these bills, even if he shouldn't have done what he did."

"I ain't got it t' pay," growled Burnell, sullenly, evidently going through a struggle within himself. "They'll have t' wait till——"

He was interrupted by a peculiar half-bark, half-cry and the sound of frantic scratching against the storm door, outside, muffled by the intervening vestibule and its two doors.

Dwight sat up as if ready to spring, his eyes dilated, his ears turned to catch a possible repetition of the sound. When it came again, it was a clear, loud bark, and it was Whitepaw's bark, unmistakably. Dwight leaped for the door, Miss Martinby right after him.

"You'll catch cold, going out like that," warned the old lady.

Dwight was too excited to hear her. Opening the door, he swung it over to Miss Martinby and reached anxiously for the storm door. As soon as the storm door was opened, Whitepaw fell upon him. His big paws on Dwight's chest, Whitepaw's hot tongue licked away feverishly at the boy's cheeks.

"Whitepaw!" cried Dwight, seizing the dog by his shoulders.

"Come in and close the door, both of you," shouted the old lady. "You'll freeze to death."

Dwight turned to obey her, seizing Whitepaw by the long hairs of the scruff of his neck; but as he did so, he saw that Miss Martinby was holding the storm door slightly ajar and looking out at a policeman and another man who were coming up the little cement sidewalk, their boots crunching the cold, hard snow noisily.

Dwight pulled Whitepaw into the living room, and Whitepaw, glad to be allowed in, went nervously,

Whitepaw fell upon him.

looking back over his shoulder as he went, his breath rising in little clouds of vapor.

Instead of taking his seat on the davenport, Dwight unconsciously sought the protection of the forceful old lady, by going toward her.

"Do you suppose they have been chasing him?" she asked under her breath, as her daughter was ushering the two men into the room, after they had shaken the house, stamping the snow off their boots in the vestibule.

Dwight was too worried to speculate. His eyes were riveted on the policeman, as he was removing his furlined cap and gloves.

"Won't you be seated?" said Miss Martinby, pulling a chair forward.

The young man with the policeman went across the room and got himself a chair and sat down, but the policeman remained standing. Putting his gloves and cap under one arm, he pulled out a notebook and pencil.

"That your dog?" he asked, pointing with his pencil at Whitepaw, but looking at Miss Martinby.

"He belongs to Dwight, here," said Miss Martinby. "Dwight lived with this gentleman, near Vermillion," she went on, nodding in the direction of the farmer, who was obviously very uneasy in the presence of the officer.

"He's *your* dog, then?" said the officer, addressing Burnell.

"He ain't none o' *my* dog," Burnell shot back, sensing trouble in the stern look on the policeman's face.

"Well, now, whose dog *is* it?" demanded the officer.

"The dog belongs to Dwight," said Miss Martinby, glancing at Dwight, encouragingly.

Whitepaw lay close to Dwight's boot, panting noisily and looking on with intense interest, as if he understood every word being said.

"You see, Dwight has been living with the Burnells, who took him out of the Edmonton Orphanage three years ago," Miss Martinby went on. "On the farm there, Dwight wanted this dog for his own. He got him as a pup. Mr. Burnell wanted no more dogs. Because of that, Dwight left his home with the Burnells and started out to Edmonton on foot—the dog with him."

"We got three dogs a'ready t' feed!" said John Burnell to the policeman, but the officer didn't appear to sympathize with him.

"I taught school up there," continued Miss Martinby. "Dwight came to Edmonton, thinking that I might be able to help him. On the way, he was caught in a blizzard and took shelter in Harry Lorwell's hunting lodge, on the Saskatchewan. Harry found him there, very sick, and brought him into town to the hospital, in his cutter. His cutter is just big enough for two to ride in and there was no room for the dog. Whitepaw followed the cutter; but when they reached the street traffic of the city, they lost him."

Dwight walked back to his seat on the davenport and sat down beside Miss Martinby. Whitepaw jumped up anxiously, at once, and trotted after him, lying down close to him and laying his muzzle on Dwight's boot. The young man who had come with the officer laughed out heartily.

"He's not going to let *you* get away from him any more," he said.

Even the policeman smiled with obvious admiration, but John Burnell only stirred uncomfortably in his rocker.

"I don't know how he managed to keep alive here in town," said Miss Martinby, "and I can't understand how he managed to find Dwight this evening."

"You been out walking any today?" asked the officer, looking at Dwight.

"Miss Martinby an' I took a little walk this afternoon," said Dwight.

"We walked to the University grounds and back," added Miss Martinby.

"That's where he picked up the scent," said the policeman to the young man; then turning back to Dwight, he said: "We followed him after we caught him at a chicken coop, stealing chickens, to find out where he lives, to whom he belongs. I'm afraid he's gotten you into quite a little trouble, son. He's not only been breaking into a chicken coop, making holes in the straw roof, but he's done other damage in town. A few nights ago, he broke into Sam Gleason's woodshed— Sam had some wild game hanging there. Sam heard him late at night and went down to see what was going on. He was carrying a lamp, and he says the dog jumped at him and knocked the lamp out of his hand. The woodshed and most of the things in it burned up. Sam's pretty mad. He says he's going to sue the dog's owner for a hundred dollars damages."

"Another hundred dollars to pay!" broke in the old lady, looking at the farmer.

"You think the law can make *me* pay all that," said Burnell, "when I didn't want the dog from the first? When I told the kid I'd shoot the critter first time he come on my place?"

"I can't tell you that," said the officer. "I'm no judge."

"Whitepaw never did things like that before," pleaded Dwight.

"We caught him in the act," said the officer. "George Harding, here, and I laid a trap for him at the chicken coop."

"He didn't know nobody," Dwight defended him earnestly. "He was hungry and he had to find something to eat."

"You're right, son," said George Harding forcefully. "I'm very much interested in this dog. I've been writing stories about him in the Register——"

"Good gracious!" cried the old lady. "You don't mean to say you think he's the wild dog the Register's been telling about!"

"I'm afraid I do," said George Harding, smiling, "at least we thought it was a wild dog of some sort doing all those things."

"That's impossible," said Miss Martinby. "Why this dog's only a pup. That's why I never made the connection. I kept him at my little teacher's house on the school grounds, for Dwight, ever since he was a tiny pup, and that was only last March. He's the most affectionate creature I have ever known."

"We wired the thatch roof of the chicken coop where he was in the habit of tearing the straw away and taking chickens out," said Harding, "and he's the fellow who set off the burglar alarm. We caught him at it. But shucks, now I understand why he did all that, alone in a strange city, no one to go to for food. I wouldn't think much of him if he just lay down and died."

"Your name is John Burnell," said the policeman, looking at the farmer, and writing in his notebook. "What is your address?"

"Vermillion," growled the farmer.

The officer closed his notebook and putting it back into his shirt pocket, said: "I'll have to take the dog. Have you got a rope?"

"No!" cried Dwight, tears filling his eyes, his fingers reaching down and fastening themselves in the long hairs at Whitepaw's neck. "He won't do nothin' like that any more!"

"Couldn't you leave the dog in our care?" began Miss Martinby.

"We'll assume full responsibility, officer," put in the old lady. "If you think it's necessary, we won't let him out of the house without a leash. If we feed him properly, he won't go breaking into chicken coops."

"Well, I guess I can do that," said the officer hesitatingly, looking from the old lady to the farmer, "but suppose they do want to sue for damages, how about that?"

"We're willing to help Dwight along somehow," said the old lady, "if Dwight stays with us. If he has to go back to Burnell's, Burnell will be responsible and he'll have to do the paying."

"I ain't payin' no such damages," cried the farmer. "I don't see why I should be made t' pay f'r a dog I didn't want."

"He's your boy, isn't he?" demanded the officer.

"He is, an' he ain't," said the farmer. "I ain't really adopted him legally yet. He's been on my place for a try-out. He don't seem t' like the home I give 'im; he didn't obey me an' kept the dog; let 'im go back to the orphan asylum."

"You needn't worry yourself about where he's going," said the old lady, coming forward. "He has a home right here."

"That's all right with me," said the farmer. "You c'n keep 'im."

He jumped up angrily, and Miss Martinby went to get his coat and cap for him.

"You better say all that in writing," said the old lady, and rushing back to her secretary, she sat down and began scratching noisily as she wrote fast and nervously.

"There," she said, finally, lifting the paper for better light, "I guess this'll do it."

She read: "I, John Burnell, do not wish to have Dwight return to my home, and I refuse to hold myself responsible for what he or his dog did."

"Now sign here," she added, thrusting the pen into the farmer's hand.

John Burnell's big hand trembled as he scratched out his name; then he turned about, seized his coat and cap and striding over to the door, hastily put them on. Without looking at anyone, he pulled down the flaps over his ears and bolted out of the door.

"Well, that disposes of him," snapped the old lady.

"I better be getting along myself," said the officer, laughing. "You coming, George?"

"I'm going to stay a few minutes longer, if I may," replied Harding. "I've got to get a few more facts about this wild dog who doesn't seem to be wild at all."

The policeman buttoned up his heavy, dark-blue mackinaw, lifting the thick woolen collar up over his neck and took hold of the door.

"Good night, everybody," he said, bowing cordially. "You folks will see that the dog doesn't get loose for a while—I know he won't be hungry, but I just want to play safe."

"You can rest assured, officer," said Miss Martinby, "that there'll be no further trouble."

The policeman bowed and walked out.

"Take off your coat," said the old lady to George Harding. "You'll be cold when you go out again."

"Thank you," replied Harding, at once removing it; and as Miss Martinby took it from him, he pulled the rocker in which the farmer had been sitting all evening closer to Dwight and Whitepaw. As he settled himself comfortably in the rocker, he took out a pencil and a pad of paper.

"Is it your father who is the editor of the Register?" asked the old lady, coming toward him.

"My father is the publisher," replied Harding. "My uncle is the editor. I like to call myself his assistant, but

I'm just a cub reporter with extraordinary privileges."

"I knew there were several Hardings connected with it," said the old lady, going off toward the kitchen.

In the doorway she passed her daughter.

"You go sit down," she ordered. "He may need to ask you some questions. I'm going to make a cup o' tea. Seems to me it's getting colder every minute."

Miss Martinby sat down beside Dwight. Harding was smiling down at Whitepaw, who was now looking up with intense interest at the reporter, his left paw resting on Dwight's boot.

"That dog fascinates me," said Harding. "He's a beautiful animal!"

Miss Martinby looked smilingly at the dog, and Whitepaw's burning eyes immediately turned to her. He knew that he was the subject of the conversation.

"Tell me everything you can about him," Harding went on enthusiastically. "I feel there's a corking good story here, if I can strain myself hard enough to write it up as it should be written."

"You go ahead, Dwight," said Miss Martinby. "Tell him just what you told me. Tell him how you took the mother dog up into the hayloft that night, when you slept up there, because I had to sleep in your bed. Tell Mr. Harding how sorry you were for the poor mother dog and all that. Tell him how she looked up at you when you took the pup in your hands. Remember that. Tell it to him the way you told it to me. You told it so beautifully."

Shyly and hesitatingly, Dwight struggled through his story, Miss Martinby helping him occasionally with a word or by putting a question to him, to bring out a point.

"You see," said Miss Martinby, "poor Whitepaw, reared in an atmosphere of the greatest kindness and care, suddenly found himself in a strange and noisy city. It must have been bewildering, terrifying!"

"Think of the devotion to Dwight, in that doggy heart of his," said Harding. "He must have been terribly afraid of the big city, of cars and people and things he wasn't used to; but he remained, wouldn't go away to the country he knew better and liked better, because he wouldn't leave the place where he knew Dwight was. What a story he could tell, if he could talk!"

Dwight looked tremulously down at the noble head.

"I'll find work," he said earnestly. "I'll pay off all the damages that's got to be paid."

"Don't worry too much about that," said Miss Martinby. "We'll find a way."

"I have an idea," said Harding, abruptly, clicking his tongue and winking amusingly in an effort to remove the worry from Dwight's peaked face. "I have written three stories so far on the wild dog; and I have sold all three of them after we published them, to the Associated Press for use in papers all over the United States. I have already gotten over fifty dollars out of Whitepaw. I think I owe *him* something, too. This story that I'm going to write tonight should be my best, and I should be able to get a great deal more for it. Whatever I get for it now will help pay whatever damages we may have to pay."

"You don't need to do that," said Dwight. "He's *my* dog; I want to pay—anyway, maybe I can pay you back later."

The old lady reappeared in the doorway with a tray, and George Harding jumped up to take it from her. Miss Martinby pulled the little serving table from the wall to the center of the room, and Harding set the tray upon it. The old lady, meanwhile, went back into the kitchen, from where she returned at once with a bowl of bread and milk for Whitepaw.

Whitepaw seemed to know at once that that was for him. He sat up eagerly on his haunches and began licking his chops, eyeing the bowl in the old lady's hands.

"Make a bow!" ordered Dwight.

Whitepaw tripped around a few moments, as if looking for the proper place; then, as Harding looked on with a broad smile, he stretched his forepaws before him, arched his back, dipped his muzzle till he touched his paws, and sprang back quickly, diving at once into the bowl which the old lady set down on the rug before him, wholly unmindful of the laughter that filled the room.

"How did you teach him to do that?" asked Harding.

"He's awful smart," said Dwight. "He can learn anything."

Harding was taking the cup of tea Miss Martinby handed him. As she was pouring the cream into the cup, he said:

"I just got a corking good idea. You insist on paying the damages, Dwight—that is, you don't want anybody else to have to pay them. I know how you feel. Why not let Whitepaw pay for his own sins? He's a smart dog. And he's a famous one, here in this town. People will be very much interested in him, when this last story is published. He has become valuable from an advertising point of view. If you could teach him to pull a cart with the Register in it, it will be an advertising for the Register for which my father will be glad to pay all the damages. You want a job. We'll give you a good route, delivering papers every morning before school. You can earn from fifteen to twenty dollars a month, depending on the size of your route. And to advertise the paper, we'll have a blanket made which he can wear as he pulls the wagon, and on this blanket we'll print in gold letters, THE WILD DOG OF EDMONTON. On his cart we can print: READ THE DAILY REGISTER. How does that strike you?"

Dwight was so overjoyed, he found it hard to answer.

"But you'll have to get up at four o'clock in the morning," warned Harding.

"I won't mind that," cried Dwight quickly. "I had t' get up earlier'n that on the farm."

"We'll see that you get plenty of sleep," put in Miss Martinby. "You'll get home from school at three-thirty. That will allow you plenty of time for your home work, before dinner. We'll fix up that front room, upstairs, for you. We'll make it real nice and cozy. And we'll put that desk I showed you in the basement into it, and I'll help you rig up a case for your books and things. You'll have things right handy and you'll enjoy doing your school work."

Dwight obviously struggled against the inclination to laugh for joy.

"I'll take care of the stoker," he said in an effort to sober up, "an' I'll shovel snow off the sidewalks. I'll go to the store for you, too, anytime, an' Whitepaw can bring home groceries and things in the cart."

"Just now you had better, both of you, get to bed," said the old lady.

"I'd better get to work," cried Harding, jumping up. "I'll be writing till two o'clock in the morning."

"Thank you an awful lot, Mr. Harding," said Dwight, standing up, one hand taking hold of Whitepaw, who had started up as soon as he did.

"Not at all, Dwight," said Harding. "This is just a plain business proposition with me."

He winked at Miss Martinby, who had brought his coat back to him.

"You must come again," said the old lady, as Harding bowed himself out of the door.

"You bet I will," he replied. "This story may take longer to write than I think—I might even make a book of it—it's got me thinking hard."

When the reporter was gone, the two women turned to Dwight whose face was glowing uncontrollably with joy.

"Be all right if I take Whitepaw up to my room with me?" he asked.

The old lady looked at him with pretended displeasure.

"If you don't ask me to let you take him into your bed with you," she said, and broke into a smile.